TAMING THE DEER DEMON

STEPHANIE M. ALLEN

CONTENTS

TRIGGER WARNINGS

- Blood & Gore (This *is* a monster romance after all)

- Emotional Trauma from a Past Relationship

- Anxiety and Panic Attacks

- Stalking

- Explicit, On-Page Sexual Content

⚜ ⚜

This book is for all the monster fudgers who watched *Hazbin Hotel* and wondered what it would be like. This is also for the Prince Cardan peeps. And even though Jude could probably kick our collective assess, we'd still shoot our shot.

⚜ ⚜

CHAPTER ONE

CHRISTINE

Yes, I know. I know it's a bad idea to be out in the forest right now. Of course I know this. Everyone knows this. But sometimes, desperate times and all that. And right now is one of those times. Because when your car gets a flat tire on the way home from a friend's house, and you're stuck in the middle of Bumfuck Nowhere, Kentucky with zero cell service, the only options are to wait around until someone drives by, or to start walking. And since I'm the smart person that decided to take the scenic route home, the odds of someone driving by are about one in a bajillion.

And so, I'm walking along this dirt road at 10:13 P.M. I'm only about three miles from home. Give or take. I think. Assuming I didn't take a wrong turn on the dirt road a few miles back because I've never been down this way, but Kathleen assured me that it would take me home. She's the one who's lived here for her entire life so I should trust her, right?

I rub my forehead as I walk. I'm in such deep shit. My anxiety is on the verge of spiraling into a full-blown panic attack if I don't focus on my breathing. "You're fine," I whisper, though there's no one around to hear me talking to myself like a lunatic. "You're fine. Breathe in. One, two, three, four." I hold my breath. "Out, three, two one."

At least my phone has enough battery for me to use the flashlight feature. And really, this situation could be a lot worse. I could have lost control of the car when the tire popped. How the hell it popped in the first place is a good question, but one that won't be answered tonight. I could have hit a deer. Or a "Not Deer".

I quickly shove that thought from my mind. Thinking of scary-ass demonic entities is *so* not what needs to be happening right now. Especially when my flashlight catches a pair of eyes reflecting from the trees across the road from me. Nope. Not going to think about the supposed deer demon that stalks these forests. The bloodthirsty one who never leaves anything behind except for the bone of the ring finger. Because that would be incredibly stupid. Nope, I'm certain those are just the eyes of a normal deer.

It's September and during the day, it's clear that fall is coming. The leaves are all those beautiful shades of red and yellow and orange. The forests all over my town are vibrant with them. It's one of the reasons I love driving along the lesser-known roads through the forests. Of course, that doesn't explain why I thought it was a good idea to do that at night when I can't see a damn thing, and my odds of hitting something and wrecking my car are super high. Then again, maybe it wouldn't have mattered considering my tire went flat and I'm stranded. Plus, I trusted Kathleen that it was a shorter, more direct route home. Boy, is she going to get an earful when I get service again.

I choose that moment to check my phone, my heart dropping when I see the circle with a line through it instead of bars. I don't know why I expected to have service suddenly. I've walked, like, a hundred feet or so. "Ugh! This blows!" I don't shout, not exactly. But my voice is a lot louder than it should be considering the only sounds around me are those of nocturnal insects and the rustling of the leaves. I tilt my head to listen. The rustling of dry leaves on the ground.

The hair on the back of my neck stands up. For those that grew up in the backcountry, it's probably common sense not to question sounds you hear in the forest. For someone like me who grew up in Dallas, Texas? For all I know, those sounds signify a deer, a wolf, a bear, a fucking vampire. Okay, maybe I'm getting a little freaked out again. Maybe I'm a lot freaked out. Because am I crazy, or is something walking toward me from the woods?

Don't shine the light over there. Just keep walking. Don't make eye contact. Ignore it. What's that saying? If you don't see it, it won't see you? Oh my god. I'm going to die out here and no one will know. Stop it!

My thoughts are a jumbled, chaotic mess as I continue walking down the dirt road. I'm walking a tad bit faster than I was a few seconds ago. Okay, something is definitely following me. Distinct footsteps crunch through the dried, crumbling leaves off to my left. And it's keeping pace with me.

Don't run. If it's a predator, it'll chase you. At least, that's what common sense tells me. But my heart feels as though it's about to crash through my ribs. My phone light is shaking with more than just the rhythm of my arm as I walk. I know I probably shouldn't, but I glance back to see how far I've walked from my car. I can't make it out. The light from my phone dimmed my vision enough that my pupils aren't adjusted. And the moon is barely a sliver in the sky.

The crunch of gravel almost makes me jump out of my skin. Holy shit, something *is* walking toward me. *Oh my god oh my god oh my god.* What do I do? There aren't any houses around here, and I was right about zero cars coming by. Well, if I'm going to go out, I might as well go down swinging. Or something like that. Fuck accepting my fate. Whoever – or whatever – is following me is about to find out that I don't give up.

I take a deep, casual breath as I turn the flashlight off. "I need to conserve battery," I say, amazed that my voice doesn't shake considering I have that feeling I get in my head right before I get hit with a panic attack. But if that happens, I'm crippled and I'll die for sure. "You're fine. Everything is fine. Just like that shirt with the dinosaur on it and the meteor falling from the sky. You're fine."

I walk for a about a minute or two, letting my eyes adjust and talking to myself the whole time to stave off the panic. I can make out the road and the woods on either side of it. I can see a small hill up ahead. And I can hear the ever-present shushing of feet in the leaves. On my right side now. There's no longer a road separating me from them. Or it. *Please let it be a "them" and not an "it"*. Although does it matter at this point?

The steps aren't getting any closer to me, so I keep my pace steady as I crest the hill. If I'm right, there should be a long stretch of road, the woods tapering...off...

Oh no. I completely misjudged a turn somewhere before I got a flat tire because I don't recognize this road at all. And it's a road that leads into even deeper forest. So I'm lost with no cell service and something following me. Well. It looks like I have two options at this point. I can turn around and face the person following me. Or I can run like hell and hope for the best.

Thankfully, I've been keeping up with my jogging habit since I moved out here four months ago because when I break into a sprint, I don't feel like my lungs are going to collapse in on themselves. I cling to my phone, unable to slide it into the pocket of my jeans while I'm running. A snorting huff sounds behind me, followed by what sounds like hooves pounding against the ground.

I'm so very dead.

I sprint down the hill and without giving it too much thought, I whip to the right, hauling ass through the trees as fast as I can. I'm only praying I don't step in a hole or slip on a fallen branch or find a nest of copperhead snakes. Because that would be just my luck. The snorting huff sounds closer behind me. Is that warm breath on my neck? Oh, fuck no!

I whip to the left and dodge between a cleft of trees. There's a skidding sound through the leaves before the pounding hooves sound behind me again. I wish I'd thought to grab some semblance of a weapon from my car. I mean, it's not like I carry weapons with me. But I'd even take coins at this point. Maybe my aim would be good enough to hit this fucker in the eye.

Something scratches at my back.

I yelp and try to run in a different direction. But my luck only stretches so far, apparently, because the toe of my Converse catches on a root. I don't fall gracefully like women do in the movies. Nope. I go sprawling flat out on the ground, the air whooshing out of my lungs with a quickness that leaves me gasping, my phone flipping end over end into the leaves. I don't even have the wherewithal to curl into a ball and brace against whatever is behind me.

I roll onto my back, desperation for air leaving me careless. And that's when I realize that I should be dead. I should be so very dead.

Because an immense, furry creature stands over me. Great, hulking breaths are coming from its open jaws. Jaws that house razor-sharp teeth are highlighted by the red glow of its catlike eyes. Glowing eyes. What the actual fuck?

The only reason I don't scream is because I still can't breathe. And maybe it's the lack of oxygen, the immense fear, the oncoming panic attack I can no longer push off, or a combination of all three. But the last thing I remember before I black out is watching the creature close its jaws and tilt its head, a clawed hand reaching for my face.

Chapter Two

CAMBION

I wish the delicate human female hadn't run. After all, it's not my fault that I'm designed to kill and maim. Can I help it if the human race makes the same stupid choice over and over again? The stories of my attacks are legendary. One would think that by now, they would've figured out that I will devour any who cross my path. And it's not as though I'm doing anything wrong. I'm following my nature. I'm acting on the impulses that creep beneath my skin, urging me to run and rip and tear and kill.

But this night feels different. I can almost taste the flicker of imminent change. I snort at my internal monologue. The human female still sleeps on my pile of deer fur. My bed. But where else was I supposed to put her? It felt wrong to lay her in the dirt like a carcass. I've been careful not to touch her, or even breathe near her, for fear of that unsettling feeling in the pit of my stomach again. The one that yanked my monstrous form back beneath the skin and brought clarification to my mind again.

I think back on the events that've transpired tonight, wondering why I feel so odd. I heard the loud pop of the tire near where I was hunting and listened as the car pulled over. I was far enough away that the human had no idea I was there. I heard her speak to herself, surprised when my lips curved into a small smile.

Humans rarely amuse me. For the most part, I find them annoying, but they're a necessary part of my survival. If you can even call it that. It feels more like the curse that it is. Cursed to be a hunter instead of a loner. Cursed to eat that which I would rather avoid. Cursed to be an intelligent being forced to interact with stupid, insignificant humans who use tools and devices I have no names for because I don't care enough to learn them. But this human's demeanor stayed my hand from leaping across the road and forcing her into the chase so I could hunt her.

Her mannerisms as she walked were utterly hilarious. I found myself drawn to her, amused by the expressions that crossed her face. I didn't like it when tinges of fear colored her scent though. I'd caught whiffs of her delectable scent as I crossed the dirt path toward her, but it wasn't bringing out the hunger that I associated with humans. It was an intriguing combination of rose petals and brambles, something I've never associated with living things in my entire existence. My brain associates humans with blood and meat.

I followed behind the rose and bramble female, something stirring in the pit of my stomach. I'm not the only Demon Forest Lord that wanders the woods of this part of the world, and the thought of another coming into my territory right then caused my hackles to rise. I was not about to share this experience with anyone, though I'd hunted with others in the past. Tonight was about me and what I wanted. And what I wanted as I watched her chatter to herself and walk up the hill – what I still want as I watch her sleep – is to find out why I feel drawn to her.

Of course, then she decided to run. I had a feeling she would. She'd shut off the light on her handheld box. I know humans have notoriously poor eyesight and I'm certain she wanted to be able to see her surroundings better. But did she have to run? It didn't take long for my demon form to claw its way to the surface, my brain melting into a puddle of goo within my skull, my eyes taking on that characteristic red glow as my antlers extended to lethal points. All I felt was the hunger driving me to hunt. To rip apart. To feast.

But chasing this human felt as though two parts of myself were warring with each other. My body craved the hunt. My jaws lengthened, my claws extended, and my saliva pooled over my tongue. But my chest started squeezing itself. My heart was doing strange things in my chest. When the human tripped and fell, my stomach lurched, almost as though I was...

Bah! Utter foolishness. This is mere intrigue. It doesn't matter that when she rolled over onto her back and I locked eyes with her, I felt something slither and coil in my chest, locking into place. Her rose and bramble scent yanked my snout backward into my head with such force, my face started hurting. My antlers shrunk deeper into my skull so fast, my head pounded for a moment. My tail twitched as her eyes rolled into the back of her head and she went very, very still.

I scrub a clawed hand down my face as I study her still form on my bed of furs. What in hell possessed me to pick her up and carry her to my cave? "Fuck," I growl, low enough that I know she won't hear. Human profanity is so useless, but even I am tempted to utter the words from time to time. What am I going to do with her? What am I going to do with myself?

She stirs a bit as I watch her. She's only been asleep for about ten minutes or so. A prickle of worry tickles my brain. Humans aren't supposed to black out for that long, are they? I wonder if she's injured. I suppose I'll find out soon enough because she's struggling to sit up. I should go over and help her.

No, you fool. She'll scream if you approach her. Humans are silly and scare easily.

Though I'm settled in my half-human form, I'm still different than she is. My antlers jut proudly from my head. My ears flick at the little noises she makes as she shifts her position – ears that are nothing like the flat things on the sides of her head. My hooves shift against the dirt a bit, though I maintain my seat.

Her eyes, colored like a deep lake, blink as she looks around. Until they focus on me. And then, whites show. Her plump, pink lips open wide as a scream reverberates through my cave, shrill enough to make my deer ears bleed.

CHAPTER THREE

CHRISTINE

I'm aware of two things as I start to regain consciousness.

One. My head hurts as though I'm developing a migraine. And two. I'm lying on something soft and furry. I run my hand over the material beneath me. Okay. I'm definitely lying on fur. Which is weird because the last thing I recall was falling in the forest. I force myself to sit up before I remember the reason why I fell.

I was running from something. But that had to be a dream, right? Because I saw...

Nope! Nope, I definitely did *not* see some kind of monster with glowing, red eyes chasing me. It was a person. Only a person. I look around the...room? Cave? Where the hell am I? The walls are made of pockmarked stone. There's no furniture. The floor is either covered by dirt or is just dirt. But all that goes through my brain in half a second. My eyes snag on the person sitting across the small space from me.

Not a person. A creature.

Antlers sprout from a head of light brown, shaggy hair. Deer ears flick up as I glimpse over the rest of its body. A...surprisingly handsome face, marred by ruby-red eyes – red but not glowing. A muscular, tanned torso and two strong-looking arms. Ripped abdominals. A furry patch on the chest that continues in a line until it melds with the fur that starts along its hip bones. Deer legs complete with hooves. Oh my god. The thing is part human, part deer, part monster, part demon, I don't even know what the fuck.

My mouth opens and I scream. Did this thing really expect anything different? I cover my mouth as my scream morphs into hyperventilated breaths. "Oh god oh god oh god. What is this?"

"Calm yourself, human."

I blink at the low, rumbling cadence of its voice as it stands. It has the gall to look irritated with me, its ears pinning back against its skull. Not it. *Him.* My traitorous gaze notices the furry penile sheath and heavy sac between his legs. I snap my eyes back up to his face. Yep. Definitely a demon or monster of some kind with those red eyes. *Yes, Christine, because the* eyes *are the odd thing about this creature.*

He hasn't moved closer to me. Of course, I don't feel calmer despite his words. I'm still breathing hard, my body inching back on the pallet until my spine touches the rock wall. I'm in the presence of some kind of "Not Deer" and he told me to calm down like I could just push a button and immediately feel better. Not that I would expect him to understand things like anxiety and panic attacks and how my brain just does its own thing when it wants to. Especially during times like right now when everything is out of my control.

"Human, you're going to faint again if you don't regulate your breathing. Honestly."

I blink at the creature, distracted by the haughty, arrogant tone of his voice. His eyes are narrowed with what I imagine is irritation. "Are you serious right now?" My voice doesn't sound normal, not by any means, but at least my brain is functioning enough for me to form words.

The creature crosses his arms over his chest. "Of course I'm serious."

"Okay, first of all, I'm sitting in a strange place with no idea how I got here so I have to assume you brought me here. Second, I'm sitting in this strange place with a fucking monster! So forgive me if I seem a little on edge!" Why is my voice getting all high-pitched and squeaky?

The creature's ears pin back against his skull again as his eyes flash. "Monster?" His teeth snap together on the word.

Very sharp teeth, I might add. "What gall to call me a monster when humans are the ones who leave trash among the trees and destroy everything they touch."

Oookaaaay. "Look, I don't know if this is some weird fever dream or what but." I don't even finish my sentence. I stand up, though my body sways a little. "Whoa."

I'm enveloped in warmth, steadied on my feet mere moments after I start to fall. "Easy, little human." The creature's clawed hands – *claws* – are on my biceps. I stand eye level with his chest and...oh boy. What a glorious chest it is. I look up, surprised to find him studying me with a strange expression on his face. Curiosity? Concern? It's hard to read when his eyes are the color of ripe strawberries.

"Listen," I breathe, my voice unsteady. My nerves are vibrating at an unhealthy frequency as I glimpse his shark-like teeth again. "I really need to understand what's happening right now because this can't be reality." And if I don't get a handle on my anxiety, I'm going to lose it more than I already have.

The creature cocks his head to the side, his ears pointing straight up. "So do I, little human." He takes a deep, huffing breath, his nostrils widening for a moment. His eyelids flutter closed. It's not at all creepy that he just breathed in my scent like I'm a bouquet of goddamn roses. Nope. Not creepy at all. "I'm just as confused as you are."

I try to back up, but his hands tighten their grip on me. Oh, so not good. Demon or not, this thing could snap me in half and crunch my bones. The legend of the Deer Demon runs through my mind again – the one where the only remains ever found are the ring finger bone. *Don't panic. Don't freak out. If he wanted to hurt you, he would've by now. Keep him talking.* "Why are you confused?" And why does my voice sound like that, I don't say.

His ear flicks, almost as though a fly landed on it. "You puzzle me." He leans his head closer to me. I resist the urge to try to back up again. Of course, his hands are still gripping my upper arms, so that's not possible anyway. "During all my cursed centuries, I've never left a human alive. But with you, it's different." He bares his teeth. "It's maddening, to feel torn between the urge to kill and the urge to..." He closes his eyes, his teeth still bared.

This is so not good. I need to keep him talking. I also need to figure out how I can get away from this thing and find my way back home. I don't even know what time it is. The cave we're in has flickering candles that give enough light. There aren't any windows, but there is a makeshift door off to my left. "Well, I'm thankful you haven't killed me yet."

He opens his eyes. "I'd imagine you are. And well you should be. I deserve your thanks for looking after you, you know."

My eyes widen. "Excuse me?"

He grins at me. "Oh, yes. Did you think it was a good idea to go traipsing along a deserted road in this part of the country? You're lucky I found you instead of one of my brethren."

"I'm lucky you kidnapped me?" My voice is louder than it should be. "I'm lucky that you took me against my will after you chased me through the woods and scared the shit out of me?"

His grip tightens on my arm, his eyes narrowing. "Careful, human."

I really should be dead, but I can't seem to stop myself. "Careful of what? Of you?" I try to back up again, but he holds me in place. "Let go!"

"Be still." His voice has lowered an octave. His chest is rumbling. Oh shit. He's growling and his snout is elongating. It's also sprouting fur. I remember the monstrosity that loomed over me when I was laying on my back after I tripped. Yep, there are the glowing red eyes I hoped were only imagined. Oh boy.

I take a deep breath, ignoring the pain as his claws feel like they're sinking into my skin. "Okay, big guy. Easy." I lower my voice, trying to keep it soothing despite the pounding beat of my heart. "I'm sorry for getting worked up, okay? I'm just a little freaked out." His snout seems to suck back into his face as his eyes dim. The fur becomes skin once again. "There we go." I reach out and put my hand on his chest, right on the patch of fur over the middle of where his ribcage would be.

He tenses, his eyes widening, as he looks at my hand.

Uh oh. Did I do something unforgivable? Fuck, I don't know what the rules are here. Might as well just go with it. "See? I'm calm. You're calm. Everything is fine."

"You're touching me."

Why does he sound so astonished? "Well, you're touching me." I remove my hand from the warm skin of his chest. "Tit for tat and all that." What am I even saying?

He lets go of my arms and turns away from me. I can't help but notice that he has a deer tail. And a very firm ass beneath it. Holy shit, am I ogling a fucking demon?

"What is your name, human?"

I focus my gaze on the back of his head before I'm distracted by his antlers. "Christine." His hair flutters a little as his ears twitch again. It looks soft. "Do you have a name?"

He turns around, his brow furrowed in confusion. "Why do you want to know?"

I put my hands in the pockets of my jeans just for something to do that won't feel awkward as hell. "Isn't it customary to give your own name when you ask for someone else's?"

"You haven't earned the privilege of knowing my name, human."

Is this dude for real right now? "Wow. You're a bit of a narcissist, aren't you?"

His full lips quirk up in a crooked smile – one I distrust wholeheartedly. "You're very brave, human."

"Why did you ask for my name if you aren't going to use it?"

He prowls a little closer again. "Do you want me to call you by your name?"

God, what a territorial weirdo. "I don't really care what you call me. But I'd like to go home now."

He's right in front of me, close enough that I can feel the heat from his body again. The smell of loamy earth and fresh grass wafts toward me. It's not unpleasant. "You want to go home...Christine?"

The way he speaks my name sends shivers down my spine. I ignore them. I also ignore the goosebumps on my arms. "Yes, I want to go home."

"Soon." He leans away. "It's not safe right now."

A thought makes my stomach sink. "But...I can go home. Right?"

He blinks, an unreadable expression crossing his face. "If you wait here, I will re-mark the boundaries of my territory. Once I do that, we will discuss what happens next."

That sounds a little ominous. The problem is, I don't have a response in mind that won't possibly get me into trouble.

His splayed hooves leave neat little prints on the dirt floor as he walks to the makeshift door. He turns to look at me before he opens it. "I mean it. Don't leave. You won't like the consequences if you do." The door wedges closed behind him.

I stay where I'm at as I count to two hundred. Not for the first time tonight, I'm grateful that I'm in jeans and sneakers. I wish I had something to tie around my hair. When the creature opened the door, I could see that it was still dark outside. He's a moron if he thinks I'm going to stick around in this pit waiting for him to come back and decide if he wants to kill me or keep me as some kind of pet.

I tiptoe to the door and pull on it. It's not sealed. A breeze washes over my face as I step outside. I don't recognize the area. It's in the middle of the woods somewhere. But I have two options at this point. Stay and wait for the demon thing to come back. Or make a break for it. I don't have my phone. It must be lying wherever I dropped it when I fell.

I listen to see if I can hear rustling leaves or heavy huffs of breath. Yep, that sounds creepy even in my head. But I'm dealing with a monster here in this new reality I've tumbled into. I'm still figuring out what the rules are. One rule I'm not going to follow though? Staying in this hovel. I wedge the door shut and sprint into the trees.

CHAPTER FOUR

CAMBION

What am I doing? I snarl, my claws cutting into the palms of my hands as I pace the perimeter of my territory. It runs for several miles in a loop, but even that may not be enough time to allow me to collect my thoughts.

This isn't like me. Humans don't make me flustered or unsure. They're prey! I liken them to the rabbits, foxes, coyotes, and deer I hunt. I eat them and move on with my life. They're food. Nothing more. Nothing less.

So why is this human female making me think of other things?

My chest tingles where she flattened her palm against it, the ghost of her touch making my fur want to puff up. My tail twitches as I remember the heat of her hand. I wanted her to slide her hand over more of my skin and fur. I wanted to lean into her touch. To press my face to her neck and inhale a deep whiff of her bramble and rose scent. My groin is starting to ache.

I snarl again as I push on my penile sheath. My cock is trying to extrude. What. The. Fuck. It did that in my cave too. I had to turn away so she wouldn't see. It's never done that. Not once. I don't feel attracted to anyone or anything. I never have in the three centuries I've been cursed as a Demon Forest Lord, losing my status as Deer Forest Lord. If I'm being honest with myself, I never felt attraction before that either, but now that a monster-of-sorts prowls beneath my skin, it seems even more far fetched to be thinking of something as trivial as mating.

Is it possible? The thought brings my hooves up short. I lean my forehead against a tree and plant my hands on either side of my head. My claws extend into the bark, giving me something to focus on besides the thought that just occurred to me. My curse is permanent. I am forever bidden to roam this small section of the forest, protecting it and keeping it in balance. It's more complicated than that, but that's the gist of it. Though my duty has changed over the decades, I've kept to my code. There are certain things I can't prevent, like humans moving onto the land. They hunt. They cut down trees to make way for more houses. They litter and are irreverent toward nature. But I handle each situation as it comes through my territory.

I accept that this is my lot in life. But there is one exception to living the rest of eternity as a cursed Forest Demon. One thing that will give me freedom to go wherever I please for however long I please. It's also the one thing that can destroy the very essence of my inner being. And I'm happy with the way things are, dammit! I don't want the status quo to change. I certainly don't want to consider the possibility that I could be beholden to another. This human...might change everything.

I retract my claws from the tree. Is my heart rate speeding up? I place one hand over my chest, dismayed to find that it is. No. This cannot be happening. *I* will not *allow* this to happen. I have to kill the human woman.

Christine.

No! I will not think of her name. I shouldn't have asked for it in the first place. I will kill her and move on. The status quo will not change. I will continue living in my territory, taking care of my forest, and helping to keep the other Demon Forest Lords in check when they overstep their boundaries.

Yes, I'll go there now and end this female. My hooves scuff against crunchy leaves as I make a beeline for my home. When I kill her, she will cease to exist, even in my thoughts. She will be forever erased from my memory. I ignore the strange cramp beneath my ribs as I plan how I will kill her. Snapping her neck would be the easiest and quickest way. And then I can eat her and leave her finger bone outside of my territory. The Fox

Demon Lord will be angry, but there won't be anything he can do about it. None of the others have close enough territory to care.

"Fuck," I snarl as something beneath my ribcage pinches. Why does it feel like my chest is squeezing in on itself? I've never felt a pain like this. Is there something wrong with my heart? It's beating just fine. In fact, it's beating faster than it ever has, even during my hunting forays. I'm almost to the cave. Then I can end this and feel better.

The human's scent lingers outside my door. That's odd. I brought her here over an hour ago. I push open the door and stop dead in my tracks. My home is empty. My brain squeezes as my snout begins to elongate. She left. Why did I trust her to stay put? I made a miscalculation. I assumed she wouldn't leave because she didn't know where she was. No matter. I'll track her. The chase will make it easier to kill her, especially because I can feel my reasoning slipping away as I give in to my monstrous beast. The space in front of me glows red with the light from my eyes.

My ear flicks as I hear a high-pitched squeal. Is that her? I can't imagine it would be another human lost in the woods at this hour. A yelping cry echoes among the trees. My ear flicks again as that same scream follows. Oh. She's being chased by the Fox Demon Lord.

My beast rips outward with a fury I haven't felt in a long time. The Fox Demon thinks to take my female for himself? All thoughts leave my head except for one as I bound in the direction of the screams and howls.

Mine.

CHAPTER FIVE

CHRISTINE

I only run until I feel like I'm far enough away that – Okay, that's a straight up lie. I stop running when I feel like my lungs are going to pop like balloons. I don't know why I'm having trouble getting a full breath in. Maybe it's because I fainted earlier. Or maybe it's the lingering anxiety and panic that may never go away at this point. I mean, it doesn't go away on a good day, but this level of anxiety may be the new normal for me. Each step I take away from the cave hovel makes my chest tighten just a little bit more. Maybe I'm having another panic attack. That would be a reasonable reaction to learning that "Not Deer" demons fucking exist!

I'm not sure how long I've been running. I never wear a watch and I have no idea where I am, let alone where my phone is or where I left my car. Okay. This was a stupid thing to do. I should've waited until morning and then made some excuse to leave. To make matters worse, I have to pee. Peeing in the woods in the middle of the goddamn night seems like the least fun thing on top of all the other not-fun things that have happened to me, but hey. My body could be sitting in the stomach of a Deer Demon right now. Best to focus on the positive, am I right?

Once it gets to the point where I'm about to piss my jeans, I take care of my business next to a tree, icked out by the fact that I can't wipe. I am not grabbing some random plant or leaf either. That's a guaranteed way to get poison ivy or something equally unappealing. I'll just have to deal with swampy jeans until I find a house and beg the people inside to let me use a phone. I'm sure Kathleen will come and get me. She better, considering she's the one who told me to take the "shortcut" home.

I smack a low-hanging branch away from my face. This blows in so many ways. For all I know, I'm moving deeper into Kentucky forest. And if the Demon Deer exists, then that means other myths and legends –

"Nope. Do not finish that thought, Christine. Just keep walking."

Of course, that doesn't help me either. I could be walking in circles. I don't know how to use the stars as a map. I'm not a fucking pirate. And the woods all look the same at night. I'm so very screwed right now and I have no idea what to do about it. Nausea is swirling in my gut and my chest feels as though it'll explode from the tension.

My eyes sting and I swipe my hand across them. I will not cry right now. I haven't cried since Justin and I broke up four months ago. I refuse to let the waterworks start now. Even if I have to walk all night, I'll come across a house or a cabin or something eventually. I just need to keep putting one foot in front of the other and ignore the chafing of my inner thighs.

The hairs on my arms rise straight up in the air. I feel like something is watching me, but I don't hear anything other than my own two feet. I stop walking, placing a hand on a nearby tree. Heavy breathing sounds behind me. You have got to be kidding me right now. What do I do? I don't think it's Deer Boy. He would've said something to me about running away. Maybe it's some nocturnal animal. Or better yet, my imagination.

I turn around slowly, my heart hammering against my ribs. I close my eyes when I see a hulking creature standing on two legs. Fuck. My. Life. This is *not* happening. I can tell that this isn't Deer Boy. There's far more fur. I don't see any antlers. The thing has a long snout with a tongue lolling out. And the glowing eyes are orange. Like fire orange.

I back up a step. It takes a step. Great. I've gone my whole life not believing in urban legends, and I've met two of them in one night. Un-fucking-believable.

I keep my voice calm and soothing, like I'm talking to some normal wild animal. "Hi there. I don't mean any harm."

A snarl rips from its chest as it crouches, lowering one massive hand, or paw, to the ground.

Well, this just keeps getting better and better. "Easy there, fella. I'm just trying to make my –"

The creature lunges at me with outstretched claws. I dodge the best I can, a yelp slipping from my lips when it manages to rake its paw down my chest. I force myself to run at a full-on sprint. I look for the path of least obstacles, but I'm in the middle of the woods. I wonder if there are any people camping nearby. Or if there's a road. I scream at the top of my lungs, hoping someone, anyone, will hear me and come help. Preferably with a shot gun.

The creature lets out some kind of weird yelp, almost like it wanted to howl but changed its mind. I scream again, hoping and praying for a miracle. I will worship whatever Deity decides to save me in this moment because that's the only chance I have. I can't outrun this animal demon and I know it. Tears sting my eyes as I scramble through the trees. The creature is only steps away. I can practically feel its warm breath on my neck, just like earlier with the other demon.

A bellowing roar sounds from far behind. Much farther than the dog thing that manages to trip me. I tumble to the ground with an *oof*, though I don't get the wind knocked out of me this time. But my ribs land on something hard and a sharp pain lances across my whole side. I scramble to find something to use as a weapon. A rock. A stick. But then the demon is on me, rolling me onto my back and pinning me to the ground.

Gnarly, reeking breath assaults my senses as it snarls above me, saliva dripping from its jaws. Orange eyes light up the furry, fox like face. Oh my god, this is it. This is how I'm going to die. I struggle, whimpering cries coming from me, but the creature has me pinned in such a way that I'm almost being crushed into the ground. I can't hear anything over the growling in its chest and throat. I cry out as claws slash over my chest again, except I know that slice went much deeper than the last one. The creature's mouth latches onto my shoulder as it presses more of its weight on me.

I'm struggling to breathe. The pain is excruciating as its teeth saw through skin and muscle. I desperately buck my hips in an attempt to get free. The creature removes its jaws from my shoulder. It's only a momentary relief because it lowers its head to bite me again.

A second roar rips through the night as something barrels into the demon on top of me. I suck in a deep breath and sit up, feeling woozy and light-headed as I do. But I watch in disbelief as Deer Boy – a monstrous, terrifying Deer Boy with glowing, red eyes – clamps his jaws onto the dog demon's throat and rips it out.

CHAPTER SIX

CAMBION

Mine.

The word reverberates through my head over and over again as I bound through the forest. I don't even know what to call this feeling that floods through my body. All I know in my monstrous state is that my human is being pursued by another. And I cannot allow him to catch her, or he will tear her apart piece by piece until there is nothing left.

Mine.

Mine to kill. Mine to eat. Mine to touch. Mine to have. *Mine.*

All-consuming rage puddles my brain into goo when I see the Fox Demon pinning her to the ground. The sweet scent of blood – *her* blood – permeates the night air. I get close enough to hear the sound of her flesh tearing and shredding in his jaws. It's enough to force my body into a launch. I slam into the furry demon, rolling him until his side thuds into a tree, his back concaved over a large root. My jaws clamp over his throat, my teeth tearing into his flesh as deep as I can. I bit down through the soft skin and rip.

The Demon Lord struggles feebly beneath me. With blood dripping from my maw, I leer down at him as I take his fox head in my hands. His neck snaps like a twig at my twist. He won't die despite my efforts and desire to see him torn apart limb from limb. Part of our curse prevents us from taking the life force of a fellow Demon Forest Lord. But it's enough for now. It will take him hours, maybe days, to replenish.

I am in his territory, but I will remove my human from here and take her back to my home. He will have no cause to follow me. He won't even remember this night since he lost himself to the blood craze.

I blink. How are my thoughts coherent? I raise a clawed hand to my face, where the glow from my eyes reflects off my skin. My deer snout is still extended. Even my claws are in their longer form. How can I have a semblance of thought when my brain should be a puddle in my monstrous skull?

A soft hiss of pain, morphing into a groan, pulls me from my ponderings. I whirl around, my ears pinning against my skull at the sight before me. My human – Christine – is injured. Her shoulder is torn to the point that her arm appears unusable. Her shirt has claw gouges ripped through it, blood leaking down her ribs. Her eyes are wide as they stare up at me, her lips parted in pain.

My monstrous form slips away as I kneel next to her, my claws retracting until only the tips are poking through my skin. "Christine."

She whimpers in response, though she doesn't shy away from me. If anything, her body seems to sag a bit in relief. But she's bleeding heavily from multiple wounds, and if I don't find a way to seal them, she will die.

I feel helpless as I watch her bleed, my hand moving of its own accord to her face so I might brush some of the hair away from her skin. I have magic, but it's meant to help me with my task of guarding the forest. I can mend trees or cause things to grow. I don't have healing powers that I'm aware of. I hate this feeling of helplessness. Rage courses through me at the thought that I can't do something to fix her.

You were going to kill her. Maybe you should put her out of her misery and eat her.

The thought stops me for a moment. I could do that. It would be simple enough. She'd disappear and none would be the wiser about what happened here tonight. But the thought is also abhorrent. I've moved my hand away from her face, but I feel the ghost of her hair tickling my finger. Even the scent of her blood isn't stirring me to hunger or melting my brain into a puddle of goo. If anything, it fuels the anger that this was done to her.

If I'm going to help her, I need to do it now. I'm running out of time, and she seems to be fading. Her breathing is more shallow and her blue eyes are closed. I have a sudden urge to see those eyes again. "I'm going to move you. I'm taking you back to my home."

There's no response. My gut clenches with an unfamiliar feeling that has me sliding my hands beneath her body, trying my best not to jostle her too much. I cradle her against me as her head lolls awkwardly against my shoulder. I might have things in my cave that will help me stop the bleeding and set her arm until it can heal. But I need to hurry. Her heartbeat sounds faint to my ears. The unfamiliar feeling pulses in the pit of my stomach again.

What am I feeling? I contemplate it as I bound through the forest in large leaps. My hooves grip the ground with surety, allowing my sole focus to be on this strange, urgent emotion. Is this what fear is? I've never been afraid in my long existence. Not once. Why should I be? None of the predators in this forest can stand against me. Even the Demon Lords cannot kill me. If they disable me, I will respawn in a matter of hours or days. But the thought of this fragile human bleeding out and dying?

A spike of urgency once again squeezes my lungs and stomach. I can't imagine why I wanted to kill this human. Certainly, this isn't pity or sympathy. I've never felt anything of the kind toward anything. Even when I've killed creatures out of mercy, I did it because I'm a Forest Lord. Creatures shouldn't have to suffer because of the hand of man. But empathy? I'm not capable of it.

And yet, as my cave comes into view, Christine's occasional whimpers of pain cause a stabbing sensation in my chest. I kick open my door and lay my human on my bed of furs. The bleeding hasn't stopped. I'm covered in the sweet scent of her blood as well. I can bathe both of us later. Right now, I need to find something to staunch the flow of her life force.

I move to the shelves that line the rock wall where I keep extra furs and various plants to satisfy my occasional craving for vegetation. I have some thin furs that I fashioned one winter when I was bored. I pull them out and go back to Christine. She is still breathing. I use my claws to rip the shirt covering her body. The blood seeps from the wounds across her chest. They are claw wounds, but they will seal themselves as long as I clean them. It's her shoulder that concerns me more.

I'm momentarily halted by the sight of her plump breasts spilling out of a tight piece of clothing that cups them. My groin aches as my cock hardens, wanting to extrude from my sheath. I growl, ignoring it, and focus my attention on the more pressing wound. Her shoulder has been torn apart. Bone shows beneath the shredded muscle.

A whine slips through my lips, startling me enough that I blink. I've never made *that* noise before. *Focus, Cambion!* I can't wrap her shoulder without some way to stitch it back up. But the wound is so bad, I don't know what to do. What should I do? If this were a tree with a torn branch, my magic would work to thread all the wood back together until the branch was whole once more. I think for a moment. She's still losing a lot of blood, her heart beating so slowly that I fear it may stop at any moment. Her pale skin has gone white.

I have to try or I'm going to lose her. I call upon my magic, willing the green threads of light to seal up the wound. To knit her flesh back together cell by cell. Plants also have cells. Maybe this will not be so different. I can feel the tendrils of my magic seeking and testing. I hold my breath. If this doesn't work, she will die.

My breath whooshes out in an exhale as her muscles begin to seal back together. Torn bits are mended and the wound is closing bit by bit. I concentrate until the last bit of skin has been regrown and the wound is nonexistent. She's still covered in blood, but there is no fresh stream pouring out.

Why does her face still seem so white? Has she lost too much blood to live? My chest quivers in panic – yes, that's what this feeling must be – as I will tendrils of magic inside her body.

If they can replenish skin cells and muscle tissue, can they not replenish blood cells too? I close my eyes as I guide the magic to the center of her chest where her heart pumps weakly. I encourage the magic to reproduce more blood cells.

The process is painfully slow, but it works. The sun has risen by the time I withdraw my magic, feeling drained and spent. But her cheeks are pink once more and that pasty-white color has turned into a healthy pallor. Even the wounds over her chest have closed. I must clean up my human and wrap her in soft furs before I can rest. I need to remove all her other clothing since it's sticky and covered in blood. It will need to be burned so it doesn't attract any of the other Demon Lords.

I've never fiddled with buttons, clips, or buckles, but once I study them, it isn't hard to understand how they work. I manage to unclip the tight clothing around her breasts once I sit her up and discover the metal pieces in the strap over her back. I'm brought up short by the sight of her freed breasts and rosy nipples. Her mounds are full and round and look so, so soft. I want to touch one. To run my nail along the tight little bud in the center and see what happens. I have the strongest urge to lower my face to them and lick them.

I grunt as my aching cock extrudes from my sheath. Shit, that's never happened before. I glance down at it, both surprised and confused how I make it go back inside. It's pink with a mushroom-tipped head. It's also covered in some kind of lubricant. I wonder if I can push it back inside. I grip it and a jolt runs through me. I try to push it in, my hand sliding down the length because of the lubricant. A groan slips from my mouth at the feeling, a tingling pleasure rocking through me.

I don't have time for this. It's just going to have to remain out while I take care of my human. Ignoring my aching cock as much as I can, I work to unbutton the human's pants and pull them off her. They won't go over her shoes, so I pull off her shoes and the cloths covering her feet. One final piece of clothing remains. It's covering her genitals. The material is flimsy and thin. I decide to just rip it since it's ruined anyway.

A heady scent wafts toward me from her genitals. I tilt my head, puzzled, and bring my face closer. I close my eyes to breathe it in better, staggered when my cock twitches with painful hardness. I want to taste her there. It's the most delicious thing I've ever smelled. My nose is inches from the apex of her thighs when I remember myself and force my face away. My human needs to be cleaned and wrapped in soft furs so her body can finish healing.

Bathing her is one of the most torturous things I've ever done. I bring in some water from a nearby stream and cut the soft fur into smaller squares. I wash the blood from her skin, all the while trying to ignore my twitching cock, which is still extruded. Something is leaking from the tip when I deign to pay attention to it. "Fuck," I snarl as I finish wiping my human down, careful to only touch her with the soft fur and only on the parts of her that are covered in sticky blood.

Finally, after what feels like a century of self-control, her skin is clean. I take another of my soft furs and cover her with it. She seems to be resting comfortably. Her breathing is even, and her cheeks are still pink. But even though I can't see her naked body anymore, my cock is still hard and aching to the point that I can't focus on anything else. Even after I clean her blood off my skin and fur, I can think of nothing else.

I move to the edge of the room, as far from her as I can get, and sit on the ground. My cock protrudes up, distracting and throbbing. More moisture glistens on the tip. I take my cock in hand and repeat my earlier motion, sliding my hand up and down. I close my eyes at the delicious feeling as tingles spread along my groin. Something is coiling deep inside as I pump my hand faster. Christine's body comes to mind. Her plump, soft breasts. The scent between her thighs. A whimper escapes me as the tension grows. I shift so I'm sitting on my knees, my hips thrusting into my hand as I fist my shaft tighter.

A growl rips from between my teeth as pleasure explodes through my groin, literally. White fluid jets from the tip of my cock in spurts, puddling on the floor and creating more lubricant with which to move my hand up and down. I hang my head as the last pulses of pleasure wring my body into a limp mess. I sink to the ground on my side, lingering tingles rippling through me and over me. My cock is no longer aching, but it's still semi-hard, only sucking partway back into my sheath.

I've never experienced sexual urges or attraction before. I'm no fool, though. I know what's happening. I look over at the sleeping human on my furs and realize that this urge to be near her runs far deeper than I've wanted to examine. Even now, I find myself crawling toward her, pulling myself up onto the furs and positioning her on her side so I can curl around her. I pull her back flush with my chest, pillowing her head on my arm. My other arm bands over her waist. My cock twitches against her backside as I cover us both with the fur. But despite the tightness in my groin, I've never felt more relaxed.

A tender feeling washes over me as I breathe in the bramble and rose scent of my human, my heart squeezing a bit. I could shove the feeling down, but I don't think I want to. Yes, this is new and terrifying. This is a part of my curse I never considered would affect me. And yet, I almost want it to. I want to let this feeling grow. For so long, I've felt empty. I didn't wish for anything different because I didn't know better. But now? This tender, yearning part of me that's awakened?

I want it to grow. I want it to spread. I want it to fill me. Because now that I've experienced a taste of it, I don't want to go back to feeling nothingness. I think the loneliness might very well kill me if it did.

CHAPTER SEVEN

CHRISTINE

I wake up without opening my eyes. Somehow, I've drifted back to consciousness with no concept of where I am or what day it is. I feel as though I've been trapped inside some kind of strange dream paralysis or something. The last things I remember are so surreal that they have to be a dream, right?

I keep my eyes closed as I try to assess where I am. My head hurts a little, but there isn't any bright light filtering through my eyelids. It must be nighttime. I'm lying on something soft. Clearly, I didn't die on the forest floor, so that's a win. But this feels like the furry pallet bed that I woke up on the last time I was asleep. Which means...

Oh shit. That wasn't a dream?

I do open my eyes then. Yep, I'm in the cave. God damn it all to hell! Why am I still here? Didn't I run away from this fucker? Oh yeah... He saved me from that other monster beast. But why did Deer Boy track me down in the first place? I try to move and realize I'm being held. Held? Oh my...

My head is not on a pillow like I thought. It's an arm. And there's another arm around my stomach. I feel nothing but fur against my skin. Oh...oh boy. I think I'm naked. I try to look at my body without moving my head because I don't want to wake up Deer Boy and make him angry. I'm covered by a blanket of fur. His arm is banded around the fur blanket, caging me against his body. His furred legs and hooved feet seem to be entangled with mine beneath the blanket.

Oh my god. I'm being cuddled by a demon. And not just cuddled. He's wrapped around me like I'm a goddamn stuffed animal or a pillow. His chin is even resting by the top of my head. Okay. Okay okay okay. Don't panic. He doesn't want to hurt me. At least, I can assume that since he saved me and...

I realize I should be very sore. The memory of the other monster's teeth ripping into my shoulder brings a ghost of pain to the joint. But there's nothing. Not even a hint of soreness. He brought me back here and he must have healed me somehow. Is it possible for demons to have magic? I swallow down my laugh. *We're talking about a Deer Demon, Christine. Clearly, reality as you know it does not exist on any level anymore.*

So why is Deer Boy cuddling me then? I can tell he's asleep. His breathing is even and slow. He twitches every so often. Hmm. I need to figure out what to do, but...I have to admit, it's kind of...nice to be held like this. Even if I am naked. I notice how clean my arm looks. Oh god. He must have wiped me down. Considering the fact that I'm naked... Yep, there are my clothes over on the floor. They're covered in brown blood.

I'm lying naked next to naked Deer Boy. So why am I not more freaked out about this? Shouldn't I be? Wouldn't a normal, sane person be? Am I sane? Either I've lost my shit and have spiraled into some sort of delusion, or creatures like him do exist and for some reason, he's decided he wants to save me and snuggle with me while he sleeps.

I shift a little, uncomfortable because I have to pee. And I'm really thirsty. His arm tightens around me. Okay, I guess I have to hold it for a little longer. His breathing changes and a whimper whistles from him. Oh, is he having a bad dream?

I've always thought of myself as an empathetic person. I also have a knack for finding people who need a bright light in their life. Well, it's more like they find me because they need someone who can be a bright spot in their life despite the fact that I deal with my shitty anxiety brain on a daily. Deer Boy is not a person. But he is sentient. And he has feelings, right? For the first time since I met him, I wonder if maybe he's lonely. I'm not sure how long demon creatures live. Has he always been alone? The way he's clinging to me, I can't help but think that maybe he is.

Another whimper sounds above my head. He jerks in his sleep.

"Hey," I soothe, rubbing his arm gently. "Hey, it's okay. You're safe."

He startles, a low growl rumbling against the back of my head.

"Deer Boy?"

The growl ceases. He takes a deep breath. Another. "Deer Boy?" His voice is raspy.

I chuckle. "You never told me your name. I had to call you something in my head." *Okay, Christine. Stay calm. Talk your way out of his house so you can go home.* Even though a contrary voice in the back of my mind is telling me that it may not be that simple.

Deer Boy doesn't move much now that I've woken him up. His heart is beating a little faster than it was. And his hand is moving in slow circles on the blanket that's covering me, right above my stomach. Oh...a little lower than that.

He hums as though he's thinking. "Cambion." His baritone voice raises goosebumps on my arm.

"Cambion? Is that your name?"

"Yes." His hand moves a little lower, though it's still atop the blanket. "I didn't think it was relevant to tell you before."

"Well, that's –" Oh my god. Did something hard just twitch against my ass? "Um...Cambion?"

"Hmm?"

"Are you, uh..." I swallow as his hand moves a little lower. Yep, there's definitely a hard cock pressing against my butt. Oh boy...

"Why are you sputtering? Speak right or don't speak."

I snort. I forgot how arrogant this ass is. "Wow. You know how to flatter a lady." I cover his hand with mine. "Stop that."

"Stop what?"

"Stop moving your hand down. It's distracting. For both of us, apparently."

"I'm not doing you any harm, am I?"

Well, dammit. No, he's not, but this is so weird and awkward and...I was thinking uncomfortable, but for some very strange reason, I don't feel uncomfortable. If anything, I feel safe. And fuck, it's not like I haven't done the one-night stand thing before. Too often, if I'm being honest with myself. I mean, for me to be comfortable waking up in the nude next to a demon? I know I've slept around, but...I shove that thought away before it devolves into a spiral.

I haven't answered him, which makes him seem to believe he can continue sliding his hand lower until it's resting right over the apex of my thighs. He breathes in deeply, his cock twitching against me again. "If anything, your scent has changed a little bit."

Nope. Not even going there. "It's probably because I have to pee."

"Oh." He lifts his arm up and scoots away from me a bit. "Take your time standing up. You should be healed, but your equilibrium might be a little off."

I grip the blanket to me and sit up. The room doesn't spin, though I do feel a little lightheaded. "How long have I been sleeping?"

He has a hand outstretched toward me, almost as though he was ready to catch me. "Not sure since I fell asleep too."

I keep the blanket gripped in my hand and move so my feet are flat on the floor. I wrap the fur around me and stand up, tucking it in to create a makeshift dress that covers me from the boobs down. It's too long, but better that then walking around in front of Deer Boy – Cambion – naked.

I turn around to face him and...oh boy. I didn't think about the fact that taking the blanket with me meant he would be laying on the pallet butt-ass naked with a hard-on that could poke my eye out!

CHAPTER EIGHT

CAMBION

Her eyes travel straight to my cock. And stay there.

I freeze, unsure what to do. I've never interacted with a human for this long before, let alone slept with my arms wrapped around one. I also just woke up from a horrific nightmare where she was torn apart by the Fox Demon Lord, and I wasn't in time to save her. Ugh. I assume that dream will haunt me for a long time to come. I'm surprised my body is geared up for mating considering. I've never had any type of sexual inclination before. My first orgasm happened a few hours ago. And now Christine is staring at my body with this strange look on her face. But my body reacted to her nearness before she started staring at me. Confusion flutters in my belly at the mixture of emotions I'm feeling.

Not to mention, I don't read emotions very well anyway – in myself or others. I've never had cause to. But I understand them on some level, I think. At least well enough to see that my Christine is also very confused by her reaction to my nakedness. Or, more accurately, my hard cock. Her cheeks have turned this lovely shade of deep pink. I can hear that her heart has sped up a little bit. She licks her lips and that does something funny to my dick. It twitches and grows a little harder. But all I can focus on now are her lips.

They're parted and they look delicious in a weird way. Is this why humans put their mouths together for kissing? I always thought that sounded gross, but looking at her lips? I can understand the desire. I want to taste her. I want to breathe in her sweet scent.

Her lovely body is covered by the fur, but I remember what it looks like. I can't resist the urge to stand and take a step toward her. She backs up and I freeze again. I don't know how to proceed now. Frustration and hunger pulse through my body, especially my needy cock. I understand the mechanics of sex, but following through with it? How does one initiate?

It crosses my mind that maybe Christine isn't on the same wavelength as me when she backs up another step toward the door, her eyes on my face. A small scent of fear wafts toward me. My chest squeezes. I don't want her to be afraid of me. I want her to mate with me. I know I'm not wrong that her scent changed. She's partially aroused. She tried to play it off, but my nose is never wrong. Maybe she really does need to relieve herself, but she also thought about mating with me, even if it was for a short time.

"I won't hurt you, Christine."

She backs up again, causing my brow to furrow in a strange way. My chest pinches again as her voice takes on a stressed note. "Why are you coming toward me?"

I will tell her the truth. I have to. Besides, lying is a pointless endeavor when it's clear what my body's intentions are. "I feel drawn to you." I tilt my head. "I want to mate with you."

"Oh god." The lovely pink color on her face drains away. "That's not going to happen, Cambion."

My name on her lips is divine. "Why not?" I tilt my head, resisting the urge to move closer to her. "Is it not clear that I want to mate with you? And I can smell arousal on you."

"What? No!"

Why is she lying to me? Is she going to reject my advances? Incidentally, if my chest doesn't stop aching, I'm going to reach inside my ribs and pull my heart from it because this is agonizing in a strange way. "Why not? You are an adult woman, are you not?"

"That's beside the point!"

"Why is your voice getting higher pitched?"

Christine sighs and pinches the bridge of her nose. "Listen. Let me go outside and do my business, and then we can talk about why you and I," she gestures between us, "are not going to have sex. Not now. Not ever." She turns around and pulls open the door. I follow her, but this seems to bother her. She doesn't turn around, but her shoulders are stiff. "Why are you following me?"

"To make sure you don't run away again." I shrug. "I thought that was obvious."

Christine halts, facing me. "I'm not going to run away right now, but I need privacy."

I cross my arms over my chest. "But you'll run away later?"

Her eye twitches in the most adorable way. "Listen, just...let me pee and then we can talk, okay? Can you just wait right there? I'm going behind that tree. You'll know if I try to leave." Her eyes dip down to my jutting cock again. "And can you, like, shove that back into your sheath or something?"

I shake my head. "It's too hard for me to do that."

"Sweet Jesus." She goes behind the tree. I hear her relieve herself before she comes back toward me. "Okay, first things first. I'm really thirsty. Is there water nearby?"

"There is a stream, yes." I feel a twinge of guilt. I have not thought about the fact that she must be hungry and thirsty. "Let me retrieve some. I also have some vegetation in my house that you can eat. There are some dandelion greens, carrots, potatoes, and other things. Eat some of that while I get the water for you."

Christine's blue eyes hold mine for a moment before she nods and walks past me to the cave, careful not to touch me or look at my cock again. I grab a bucket I keep outside the cave and fill it with fresh water. When I come back, I see she's eaten some of the vegetation. Good. I can't have her getting weak on me.

She eyes me as I come inside and set the bucket down next to my bed. Her eyes dart to my cock before she looks away. I smirk. She can deny that she wants me, but her body language tells me differently. Still, I cannot force this upon her. Just the thought makes me ache, and not with need. I want her to want this as much as I do.

I'm thrust into a momentary self-reflection, something I don't do very often. But my life has been turned upside down in the last six hours, irrevocably so if I'm right. I don't think there's a way to reverse this desire I have for Christine. And now that I've brought myself to orgasm, my body craves it again, but not from my hand. All I can think about is exploring the different planes of this female's body, both inside and out.

Chrisine uses her hands to cup water from the bucket so she can drink. After ingesting several mouthfuls of water, she takes a moment to adjust the fur around her body. Her gaze holds onto mine as she opens her mouth to speak.

Chapter Nine

CHRISTINE

"Okay, Cambion. I think we need to have a serious discussion about expectations. Both yours and mine."

Deer Boy nods as he sits down cross-legged on the floor. God, his erection is so fucking distracting. It looks like a man's dick, but it's also way different. It's pink and it looks wet. I know that certain animals have a natural lubricant around their penises. Maybe his is similar to that. I'm almost dying to touch it, just to see. And it's been a few months since my horny ass had sex. A girl has needs, you know? But Cambion is...not...human.

My cheeks feel hot as I bring my gaze back to his strawberry-tinted eyes. He has this arrogant little smirk on his face, probably because I can't stop looking at his anatomy. "Let me ask you this." Distract from me. Distract from my actions. "Tell me, exactly, what you want from me?"

"Forever? Or in this moment?"

I blink. "Right now. Let's just stick with right now."

"I already told you. I want to mate with you. I want to explore your body, something I've never done before." He shifts his hips, looking uncomfortable for a moment.

I imagine his cock must ache with how long it's been that hard. "Okay, but sex isn't something that you just declare you want to do, and then jump right in."

"No? Don't humans copulate with anyone they please?"

Well shit, he has me there. "Look, the thing is...you aren't..." I sigh. I have to remember that he has the capability to hurt me. Anything I say could trigger his anger and make his beast-monster-side come out. He's looking at me with this strange expression on his face. I can't tell if it's curiosity or what. "You aren't human."

He nods. "Did we really need to discuss the obvious? I'm a Forest Lord."

I'm not even going to dig into that one right now. I try a different approach. "I doubt we'd be compatible, Cambion." And I'm not even talking about the fact that he probably can't get me pregnant.

You have an IUD anyway, so it wouldn't matter if you did have sex.

Okay, intrusive thoughts need to butt the hell out.

Cambion sounds genuinely confused. "Do you not think it will fit?"

Oh boy. "This is a complicated issue and –"

He's suddenly in my space, one hand on the furs on either side of my hips. His face is millimeters from mine. All I can smell is that deep, forest scent. It's calming and soothing. It's drawing me in, and I almost can't help my reaction. Yes, he has sharp teeth, but his lips are so damn kissable. And though I loathe to admit it to myself, this handsome deer demon is turning me on with his innocence and obvious desire to fuck me.

"Wait." I place my hand on his chest. That was a mistake because now I can feel his pounding heart. *Is he...nervous?* "You said you've never done this before?"

He shakes his head. "No, I've never had the desire to mate with anyone before, human or otherwise."

"So you've never even kissed anyone? Touched anyone?"

"Just you."

Right. He bathed me. I have to ask. "You promised me honesty. When you bathed me, did you –"

His red eyes are earnest as he shakes his head. He's still kneeling in front of my legs, his hands pressing down on either side of my hips. "I did nothing beyond what was necessary to get the blood off your skin and make sure you were healed."

I sigh. I believe him. I do.

He sits back on his hooves, still kneeling. "I have never felt this way before. It's like my body has awakened to something that didn't even exist. I don't know how to explain it." His face is so close that his nose grazes mine. "All I know is that I long to feel your skin on mine. I ache to be touched by you."

My core throbs at his words. So. Not. Good. "But if –"

His lips brush mine. Shivers ripple across my body, goosebumps breaking out all over my arms. His mouth is tentative, and I feel him trembling. Perhaps he's more nervous than he's letting on. And damn, his mouth is so soft. His kiss is actually really sweet. I kiss him back, keeping my lips gentle.

A growl rumbles in his chest as he kisses me harder, mashing his lips against mine. His inexperience is clear, but he isn't lacking in passion.

My mind wanders to Justin for a moment. Justin, who often treated sex like it was chore. Justin, who inadvertently shamed me for wanting to make love with him more than once a week despite the control he tried to exert over me. And here is this male who is eager to please even as he fumbles around my mouth. He hasn't tried to touch me yet, either.

I glide my tongue along the seam of his lips. He startles against my mouth before opening for me. I take my time exploring his mouth, careful of his sharp teeth. It doesn't take long before his tongue is tangling with mine and a low, sexy as fuck groan slips out of his mouth.

I'm in so much trouble.

CHAPTER TEN

CAMBION

These sensations are breathtaking. Mind numbing. It never occurred to me that tongues could be such sensuous things. And yet, as Christine and I explore each other's mouths, I find my cock pulsating a little with how turned on I am. I'm careful not to close my teeth down on her tongue. I know I was able to resist the blood craze before, but with how heightened my senses are right now, I don't trust myself to taste her blood and not lose myself to the demon.

I don't want to hurt her.

The realization almost breaks me out of my lust-filled haze. I, who has never had any inclination of care toward another being, don't want to hurt this female. I don't want to make her bleed because I accidentally cut her with my teeth. I haven't grabbed onto her like I want to because I don't want to slice her with claws that don't fully retract. I don't kiss her as hard as my body craves because I don't want to bruise her sweet, tender lips.

I can't hurt her. I would never forgive myself. And that's saying something because I have never felt guilty for anything in my entire long-lived life.

Christine breaks the kiss and sits back, her sapphire eyes full of questions. My heart thumps hard in my chest. I don't want to stop. I don't want to separate myself from her presence. I want nothing more than to mate with her and curl up with my head in her lap while she runs her fingers through my hair and gives gentle caresses to my ears. I want her to grab onto my antlers while I feast between her thighs. I don't even know what it's called, but I know human males do that to their females.

Sometimes humans decide to mate out in the forest, and I'd be lying if I said I didn't watch from a distance with both fascination and curiosity. But I never wanted to experience it for myself. Not until now.

I'm not sure what expression is on my face. I've never considered that my thoughts can be read from my eyes, the angle of my head, my ears, my mouth. But Christine's gaze seems to soften, melting until I see tenderness. Her little hands come up to cup my face. I have to fight back a full body shiver as her thumbs brush against my cheeks. "Cambion?" Her soft voice sounds tentative. "Are you sure you want to do this?"

I swallow against the sudden lump in my throat. "Yes, I do."

She hesitates, her flat teeth biting into her lower lip, which is a little more swollen than it was before. "I just need you to understand that after we do this, I –"

"It doesn't matter," I interrupt. I don't care what she's going to say. I just want to know if she's willing to mate with me. "As long as you want to mate with me, nothing else matters."

Christine sucks in a shaky breath. "Are you sure?"

I close my eyes at the sensation of her thumbs caressing me, imagining how they will feel on other places. "Yes." I can't help the moan that slips out as her hands slide to my chest. She kisses me again, sending more shivers over my whole body. Maybe I should be embarrassed by the sounds coming out of me. By the way my heart is thundering in my chest, beating so hard that I'm vibrating with it. Surely, she can feel it beneath her soft hands.

I dare to place my hands on either side of her face, careful that my claws do not touch her eyes. I mimic the motion of moving my thumbs over her cheeks. My hands slide down to her neck. And then her shoulders. My tongue twirls around hers as I grip her arms and lift her a little, breaking the kiss again. She gasps as I lay her on her back and climb over her. I need to be closer to her, on level with her.

I resume kissing her, my fingers tangling in her soft, dark brown strands of hair. I can't help the slight thrust of my hips against the apex of her thighs. I groan at the barrier of the blanket separating us from being skin to skin. I want nothing more than to press my aching cock into that area where the scent of her arousal is so strong. But there's something else I want to do first.

"Christine," I murmur against her lips. "I want to taste more of you."

She nibbles my bottom lip, drawing a gasp from me. "Isn't that what you're doing?"

"I mean more of you," I manage to choke out, my voice guttural.

Her blue eyes sparkle as she looks at me. "Where would you like to taste me, Cambion?" Her finger traces along the edge of my ear. My cock twitches in response. It almost feels like I'm close to spilling again, but I don't want her to stop touching my ear.

"Everywhere," I groan.

Her lips curl into what I imagine is a teasing smirk. "Can you be more specific?"

So she wants to play? I give her a salacious grin and push off her enough to unbind the blanket from her chest. I let the sides fall to the bed so she is bare before me. "I want to taste you here." I kiss her neck, my tongue darting out on instinct. Oh fuck me, she tastes amazing. Sweet and salty at the same time. "And here." I trail my lips down to her breasts.

"Okay." Her voice has gone all breathy and soft.

I cup her breasts in my hands and slide down her body a little further so I can taste the rosy nipples that are peaking. I suckle on one, encouraged when I hear little moans escape her mouth. Her nipples must be sensitive like my cock. I twirl my tongue around the bud. It becomes even more taut. I switch to the other nipple, using my thumb to continue teasing the one my mouth was just on.

But I am impatient to go lower. I keep my hands on her breasts as I kiss my way down her soft stomach to a triangular patch of hair at the center of her pelvis. I grip her hips as I breathe in deeply. I can almost taste her arousal on the air. I part her thighs, and the scent slams into my nose. My pupils must be dilated because the dim room brightens a bit.

"Can I taste you here?"

She's panting as she answers. "You want to eat me out?"

"Yes." I graze my nose against the curly hairs as I pull her thighs farther apart. "I want to lick these pink folds." So many layers, all of them glistening with juices I want to lap up with my tongue. "I want to suck on this right here." I press my nose against a small bud that looks like a nipple at the apex of her thighs.

She lets out a yelp. "It's called...a clit."

I separate her folds and lick her from the bottom to the top, stopping at her clit. "I don't care what it's called," I murmur against her as I suck it into my mouth. Her hips buck against my face, and I'm lost to the magnificent taste of this woman as I feast on her.

CHAPTER ELEVEN

CHRISTINE

I've had a decent number of sexual partners in my twenty-six years, though my first boyfriend didn't come along until I was nineteen. Since then, I've had a few "one and done" nights. I've had short term boyfriends. In the last year, I've been with only one man though – Justin. But none of them – and I mean *none* of them – ever went down on me the way Cambion is now.

Deer Boy is feasting on me like he's starving in the desert and I'm the oasis he found. Okay, that's a bad analogy, but you know what I mean. My first boyfriend went down on me a few times in the eight months we were together. He was decent at it. I came once or twice from his tongue, although he seemed to get bored pretty quickly. Justin only went down on me once, and it was only for a few minutes at that. His one comment consisted of a partial apology while basically saying that he hated the way I tasted. None of the other guys did.

When Cambion suggested eating me out, I did my best not to tense up. I know he's a virgin and this is his first experience with anything sexual, so I didn't want to freak him out. But the way he's licking at my pussy and sucking on my clit? God, I might as well have never had anyone go down on me before.

Insecurity kicks in, and even though I've got my hands in my hair and am writhing like I'm being electrocuted, I have to ask. "Do you...like do...doing that?"

He growls and grips my hip tighter, his claws pricking my skin. His other hand holds my folds open.

"Is...is that a yes?"

Cambion slows down, tonguing me in one, languid stroke from the base of my pussy to my clit. "Christine." His voice rumbles against me, vibrating in a way that makes me moan. "If I could survive on your juices alone, I would every day for the rest of my existence."

Holy. Shit. "I don't taste...bad?"

He lifts his head a bit, his red eyes holding mine. I almost come at the sight. "You are divine, my goddess. I would worship your folds every second of every hour."

"Oh..." My back arches as he swirls his tongue around my clit. "By the way, you...you don't need to...call them 'folds'.

It's...a pussy. Or a...a cunt." I'm so distracted, I don't even pay attention to what I'm saying.

"Mmm. I like the word 'cunt', my goddess."

His tongue leaves my clit, and I almost cry out in protest. Until it slides inside me, and my hips buck as he tongue-fucks me. "Oh god. Oh. Cambion. Fuck."

"You like that?" His teeth prick me as his tongue slides deeper. The pinch, mixed with the pleasure, drives me even closer to the edge.

"Yes! Oh god, yes." I grab onto his antlers, not intending to do anything but hold on.

He chuckles. "What if I do...this?"

I feel pressure on my clit as his tongue enters me again, and I about come off the bed, no pun intended. He must be using a knuckle because I feel no prick of a claw. If I weren't in a cave in the middle of a forest, I would be embarrassed with how loud my moans are. "I'm so close! Cambion!"

He jiggles my clit in response, which sends me spiraling into a fog of bliss. I scream as I come hard, my hands gripping his antlers like they're a steering wheel, my legs shaking, as Cambion plays with me through my orgasm, drawing it out. I don't even know how long I come for. I only know that at some point, Cambion slows down, licking me in languid strokes again. It's almost as though he's lapping up every bit of cum from me.

"Divine," he rumbles. "I never imagined."

I want to sit up, but my body feels like a limp noodle. "That was... You've really never done this before?"

His eyes meet mine, a devilish twinkle in them. "Never."

I cover my face with my arm, still trying to recover. "You're very good at that."

A beat. Two. "Would you like me to do it again?"

I sit up then. "Not right now." This is another first. I've never had a lover interested in giving more than he's getting. "I think it's my turn to play with you." He hasn't moved from between my legs. "Would you like that?"

He sits up a little, his cheeks pinking in the most adorable way. He shifts his hips at the edge of the furs.

"Cambion?" I feel my face fall a little, wondering if I did something wrong.

Deer Boy doesn't meet my gaze. "I...made a mess."

Realization hits me a moment later. "Oh." *Do not laugh. Don't embarrass him.* "It's okay if you came. This is all new for you." I reach down to his soft ear and trace the edge. It flicks a little under my touch.

He closes his eyes. "My cock is still hard even though it's sitting in a puddle of my seed."

I put my fingers under his chin and tilt his face up so he's looking at me. "Cambion, do you want me to make you come again?"

He nods, his eyes earnest. "I want to feel your hands on my cock more than anything." He doesn't hold my gaze for long though. It's clear he feels vulnerable and ashamed. I can guess why, but I wish he didn't. It makes my core tremble to know he was so turned on just by making me come.

I scoot back and pat the furs next to me, smiling at him. I still feel like I'm floating a bit. "Come sit here, Deer Boy." I keep my voice lighthearted and fun.

He rolls his eyes, but I see a cute little smile on his handsome face. He crawls up and sits next to me. Sure enough, his cock is still rock hard. It's tempting to wrap my hand around it and go to town, but I want to make his first time mind blowing, so to speak. I shift so I'm straddling his lap, his cock pressing against my stomach.

His eyes widen a little, the only sign that he's nervous. Although his chest vibrates a pounding rhythm. I place my hand over a rock-hard pec as I lean in and kiss his cheek. "I want you to enjoy this." I kiss his jaw. "I want you to savor this." His hands move to rest on my hips. "And I want to make this so good for you, Cambion."

His breathing is harsh, a slight tremble rippling through his body. But his face is composed, his eyes soft as he holds my gaze.

I falter a bit. I don't know what he expects to happen after today. If he thinks I'm going to live in the forest with him in a cave like some wild woman, he has another think coming. But the way he's looking at me...

Nope. Not going there. I put pressure on his chest. "Lie back for me."

He obeys, though his hands go to my breasts and cup them, squeezing lightly.

I kiss my way down his chest, letting my fingers play in his fur. After a moment, I divert and sit up. I pick up his arm and flip it in a gentle motion so his palm is facing up. I kiss each finger tip, careful of his claws, and move my lips over his palm to his inner wrist. He shudders beneath my touch. "You good?" I ask.

"It feels...delightful." Based on the way his teeth are gnawing into his lip, I would say he's probably feeling more than that. I just smile and continue kissing along his arm to the crease of his elbow. He shivers again, especially when I repeat the process along his other arm. I hesitate for a brief second as I glance at his stomach. His abs morph into fur, and it reminds me that he is not human, no matter how much he longs to please me or how much he turns me on.

What does that say about me?

I shove the thought aside and kiss my way along his fur until I get to his pink cock. His whole body tenses, his hands moving to cover his face.

"You good, Deer Boy?" I keep my voice light, trying to convey that I'm enjoying myself and letting him know it's okay to feel the things I'm sure he's feeling.

He chuckles, breathless. "This is...beyond words."

I decide to taunt him a bit. I slide my fingers along his fur until I reach the base of his shaft. It twitches, precum leaking out despite the fact that he came already. "This looks like it hurts." I let my fingernails graze up his cock to the mushroom head, where I finally wrap my hand around him. They don't quite reach all the way around, he's so damn thick.

A whimpering whine leaves his mouth as I glide my hand up and down, taking my time. His cock is lubricated and smooth aside from the head, which has fascinating little ridges along it. He's larger than any of my previous lovers, but not so large that I'm scared. If anything, I'm getting more and more turned on as I think about him fucking my brains out.

Focus, Christine. There will be time for that.

I take my time stroking him over and over until his hips start thrusting into my hand. He's no longer covering his face. He's watching me, intensity mixed with...adoration in his eyes. I don't know how else to describe what I'm seeing, but I see it. Before I can get lost in his gaze, I lean down and take his cock into my mouth.

He hisses as I suck him in as deep as I can. I wasn't sure what I expected, but it wasn't this. His taste is...indescribable in a way. A little salty. Somehow, there's some sweetness there. There's also a male musk that makes me moan around him. I bob my head up and down, taking him until he hits the back of my throat. I make sure to glide my tongue over those ridges, imagining how they'll feel inside me. My pussy walls clench at the thought, more slickness coating me.

"Christine. Stop." His voice is husky, growly.

I stop immediately, looking at him with brows raised. "Of course. Is it too intense?"

"I don't want to spill in your mouth." I let out a startled yelp as he sits up and flips me onto my back. His hips are wedged between my thighs, his cock pushing against my entrance. "I want to be inside you, like my tongue was." He kisses me with a sweetness that makes my heart melt. "Can I mate with you, my goddess?"

I kiss him back, so turned on I might push on his hips if he doesn't come inside me soon. "Yes. I want you to."

He groans against my neck as he thrusts his hips forward just a little. The tip of his cock teases my pussy. I wiggle my hips beneath him, but he doesn't press forward. Instead, he raises himself up enough to take both of my wrists in one hand. He holds them above my head while his other hand goes to my face. My heart flutters as his red eyes pierce mine with an intensity that steals my breath away. "You're mine."

CHAPTER TWELVE

CAMBION

She's mine.

I feel it in the depths of my languishing soul as I push my cock inside her tight heat. She closes her eyes as her lips part, almost as though she can't suck in a breath. I have her wrists in one hand, holding her in place, as her cunt squeezes my cock. I fear I have just formed a new addiction, because I will never want to go a single day without feeling this.

I lean down to kiss her, keeping my hand on her cheek, as I pull out and thrust back in. I want to move slow. I want to savor this. But my body desires to pound into her. I'm trembling with the exertion of holding myself back. Gone is my shame at spilling my seed on the fur while I was feasting on her. Gone is my trepidation and my anxiety. No, I only feel an overwhelming desire to fuck her as hard as my hips will allow. To claim her as mine. Forever.

My forehead presses to hers, my hand holding her shoulder, as I thrust into her over and over, letting instinct take over. To think I've existed for centuries and not known this pleasure. That I have the ability to lose myself in someone else, to give and take pleasure until both of us are breathless and sated. My hips move faster, chasing the moment of release that's coiling tighter and tighter inside me.

My heart squeezes as I lift my head to look at the perfect woman below me. Her beautiful sapphire eyes are closed, her full lips parted in breathless pants. Her silky, chestnut hair is strewn around her shoulders. Her cheeks are flushed. Her cunt is tightening around me. I wonder if she needs me to play with her clit so she can come again.

I push aside instinct long enough to release her wrists and move my hand between us. I shift so I can reach her clit with my knuckle. Her hands move to my ass, squeezing and pushing me against her hips. I groan into her neck as I flick her clit over and over while thrusting. When she comes around me, she squeezes me so tightly that I can't help but follow her over the edge, ramming into her with enough force that her body bows beneath me. Both of us moan our mutual pleasure as my cock pulses inside her, the intensity so high it steals my breath from my lungs.

I keep my face pressed into her neck, making sure I don't crush her with my weight. My orgasm leaves me tingling, content to remain on top of her. One of her hands moves to my shoulder while the other caresses my back in soothing strokes. I breathe in her scent, unwilling to move away from her.

She glides a finger along the edge of my ear again. "Did you enjoy that, Cambion?"

I kiss her neck before lifting myself up so I can meet her beautiful blue eyes. "I did. You are truly my goddess, Christine."

Her breathing starts to even out, her body relaxing underneath me. "Me too."

Pride fills me as I smile at her, withdrawing my softening cock from her. It finally slides back into the sheath, though I imagine it wouldn't need much encouragement for another round. I kiss her forehead. "Good." I want nothing more than to curl my body around her and sleep. Even as I study her, her eyelids droop a bit. Without a word, I shift us so her back is pressed against me, just as it was earlier this morning.

She doesn't protest as she pillows her head on my arm and shifts her backside until it fits snugly against me. "I'm so...sleepy."

I kiss the top of her head before resting my chin above it. "Then sleep. I've got you. You're safe."

It doesn't take long for her breathing to deepen and her heartbeat to slow to a sleeping pace, even though I haven't stopped letting my fingertips move over her stomach and hips in soothing motions. For the first time that I can remember, my body feels relaxed. There's no pressing hunger or other needs driving me to want to be anywhere but right here.

"Mo anam cara," I murmur against her hair. Even as I speak the words aloud, I can feel the strings strengthening around my heart.

CHAPTER THIRTEEN

CHRISTINE

When I wake up, my body feels as though it's been sleeping for a long time. That may or may not be true. Glancing around, I'm reminded that there are no windows, and I am in a cave on a pallet of furs. The pleasant soreness between my legs is another reminder of where I am and who I'm with. I'm a little hungry and thirsty, but contentment is my main emotion.

For all of six seconds.

Anxiety starts to swirl in my stomach. I can't tell if Cambion is awake or asleep. His chest rises and falls against my back. I need to go home. Kathleen will be worried about me. I'm sure my mom has tried to call me multiple times, especially if she's talked to Kathleen. I don't know if it's dark or light outside, but I know I've been missing for close to a day, if not longer. I have a burner phone at my house that I can use. And I really, really want to shower. Good thing I'm not scheduled to work until Tuesday. I'm guessing it's Monday afternoon or evening. My thirst is making itself more persistent. And I have to pee.

So what am I going to do about Deer Boy?

Anxiety rips through me again, If I'm not careful, it's going to throw me into a full-blown panic attack. I know what I saw in his eyes while we were fucking. I'm pretty sure he has some feelings blossoming in that furry chest of his. I should've expected it, especially since he's never had any type of sexual inclination before. Feelings are a bit inevitable in a situation like this I would think.

I haven't even examined what's going on inside of me, yet. My legs are tangled up with his. With his *deer* legs and *deer* hooves. This male isn't even human! What have I done? Does this make me a freak? I close my eyes against the burning sting. I don't feel shameful. Not exactly. But I'm mixed up inside. My chest is pinching in on itself and my stomach is so tight, I can't suck in a breath like I need to.

"Hey." His voice, gravelly with sleep, is soft as his lips brush the top of my head. "What's wrong, love?"

I ignore the nickname and try to suck in a breath. "I need to go home. I...I have people who are worried about me. And I've got to get my car taken care of. I have to be at work tomorrow. I have –"

He chuckles, his chest rumbling against my back. "Easy, little human. One thing at a time."

I sit up, expecting him to pull me back against him, but he doesn't. I feel a little flustered that I'm butt-ass naked, but then again, he did have his face buried in my lady bits, so I suppose modesty is out the window at this point. I turn around as I try to tame the snarls of my hair with my fingers. The smug grin on Deer Boy's face tells me he is probably thinking about things he shouldn't be because I have no intention of continuing this weird dynamic between us.

Don't you, though?

I inwardly snarl at my intrusive thought and open the door to the cave. After doing my business (what I wouldn't give for some toilet paper!) I head back inside to find Cambion soaking a soft-looking square of fur in the bucket of water that I was about to drink from. He hands it to me with a grin. "I would imagine you want to clean yourself up a bit."

I grimace because yes, my thighs are sticky. "Thank you."

He turns his back to me and starts fiddling with the pile of blood-covered furs that I assume are from when the other demon attacked me. I notice my clothes are also mixed in. Is he...giving me privacy? Huh. I clean myself to the best of my ability before tossing the rag onto the pile of dirty things.

"I will take care of these later." When he looks at me, I can't gauge what's going through his mind. His expression is neutral, though his eyes are bright. Wait...they seem more...pink than red. What?

"Hey, do your...do your eyes change color?"

He shakes his head. "Not that I'm aware of. Why?"

I take a step closer. "They just seem less strawberry-red today."

Cambion chuckles. "Perhaps it's your imagination, little human." He crosses his arms. "First thing's first. We need to get you back to your vehicle. I would venture it's still sitting where you left it last night."

It's only been one day? I sigh and work on detangling my hair again. "I need to figure out how to get my tire changed. I don't have a spare right now. I let my best friend borrow it. So even though I only sort of know how to change a tire, there's not much I can do for my car unless I drive it on a flat, which is bad for the rim. And –"

A finger presses against my mouth. "Then we leave your car, and I take you to your home a different way."

I raise a brow at his presumption. "What do you mean you'll take me? I'm capable of walking home on my own. Once I find my car, I can backtrack to the wrong turn I took and walk home."

Deer Boy scowls at me as he crosses his arms over his chest. "You are not wandering the forest alone with no clothing and no protection. Did you not learn anything when you ventured out against my command last night?"

I sigh. "Fair point, I suppose. Although I'd like to know how I've never run into a 'Not Deer' before and then last night, I have the bad luck to run into two of you."

"Tell me the last time you went for a late-night walk in the middle of the woods?"

I glare at his smug look. "Whatever. Can you lead me back to my car? I can find my way home from there."

"I don't need to lead you to your car. I will simply take you home."

"No, you won't."

"Why are you acting like you have a choice?"

Right. He's a demon, Christine. A monster, for all intents and purposes. I poke him in the chest. "What makes you think I'm letting you follow me home?"

Anger flashes in his eyes. "I will escort you home like the protector I am. Once you're home, we can make any further decisions then."

"We?"

"Yes."

Oh boy. I was right. Deer Boy does have attachment issues happening. This is so not good, but it's not something I can address right now. Apparently, he's coming with me whether

I want him to or not. "Fine. You can escort me home and *we* can figure out our next steps, okay?"

"Good." He approaches me with his arms out.

I back up. "What are you doing?"

He tilts his head, confusion flickering over his features. "Carrying you. What does it look like?"

"Um, no." *Uh oh. Did I hurt his feelings just now?* There's a small change in his eyes. I don't even know how I caught it. "Tell me why you want to carry me?"

"I can run faster than you can."

Ah man. I definitely hurt his feelings. His expression is neutral again. Closed off. I rub my forehead, realizing this is far more complicated than I ever wanted it to be. "Okay. Carry me then. But how will you – eek!" Before I can finish asking him how he'll get me home, we're out the door and he's bounding through the woods.

I'll admit, there's something comforting about being held. Even in this fucked up situation – with me being nude and carried by a Forest Demon – the way he's cradling me against his body is nice. He's warm and solid. Much stronger than he looks. I don't worry that he's going to drop me or stumble. He's so sure-footed and steady as he lopes along an invisible pathway through the trees.

After a few minutes, I see my car through the trees. He stops out of sight of the road and sets me down. An involuntary shiver runs down my spine as he leans close and whispers, "Retrieve what you need and then I'll continue carrying you home."

I ignore the goosebumps peppering my arms, and glance up and down the road to make sure I'm not about to cause a riot because I'm walking out of the woods with no clothes on. Thankfully, I didn't lock my car because I'm just now remembering that my keys are in my jeans, and I don't want to ask Cambion to go back to his cave so I can retrieve them. Good thing Dad always taught me to keep a spare house key under the potted plant by the front door, too.

I open my door and check the center console. See, what people don't realize is that out here in Kentucky, most of the residents won't bother your stuff. Oh sure, there's the occasional dick who will break into a car and look for drug money to steal or something. But in the surrounding towns, people are quicker to return a wallet than take it for themselves.

Unfortunately, I apparently had the good luck to encounter one of the few assholes who wanted to steal because my wallet and my spare cash is gone. Well, shit. It's my own damn fault for leaving my car unlocked. Wait...

I frown as I scour my car. My overnight bag that I usually keep on the backseat is also gone. Huh. A stray thought hits the back of my mind, but I shove it aside. There's no way in hell Justin came looking for me in Bumfuck Nowhere, Kentucky, and just happened to find my car on the side of some out-of-the-way dirt road. Besides, he didn't exactly give off stalker vibes the last time I talked to him. More like...slightly concerning, obsessive vibes. Which actually did have me wondering if he was going to start stalking me. Especially considering the fact that he was very intentional when he told me that he wasn't going to let me break up with him. But that's neither here nor there.

"Something the matter, little human?"

"Gah!" I hit my head on the sloping edge of the car door frame. "Don't fucking sneak up on me like that? Aren't you supposed to be out of sight?"

"You seem disturbed." He glances over my shoulder. "Why have you not retrieved what you need yet?"

I suppose my breathing is a little erratic. Damn these stupid anxiety attacks. I kneel on the front seat so I can check the back floor, sucking in deep breaths. "Because my stuff has gone missing."

There's a pause before I hear a low rumbling. "Another human took your belongings?"

I turn to face Cambion, surprised when I see his teeth bared. "Easy. It happens, and I'm the dumbass who left my car unlocked." I place a hand on his chest. "Let's just get to my house and I'll sort it out later, okay?"

He nods, though his body language is tenser than I've ever seen. His ears are pinned against his skull and his antlers seem to have expanded a bit. His eyes aren't glowing though. Yet. He holds out his arms and picks me up. "Which direction to your home?"

I glance around, still not recognizing where I am despite the fact that it's still light out. That means it's been less than twenty-four hours since I disappeared. And yet it feels so much longer than that. Maybe because so much has happened that I'm still trying to wrap my mind around it all. "Let's backtrack that way and then follow the dirt road."

"As you wish."

CHAPTER FOURTEEN

CAMBION

I follow Christine's directions as we travel, staying out of sight of the road. When we reach the quiet street where her home resides, I advise her to wait until it grows dark before she goes inside. Not only am I risking being seen, but the thought of anyone else seeing her bare, beautiful body makes me want to rip out a throat or two.

Of course, she doesn't listen and runs from the woods across the sloping grass hill behind her home. My chest rumbles with my displeasure as I follow. I haven't spent much time observing humans, but I do know they are nosy. I also know that it will be difficult to explain away my appearance if a neighbor happens to see me. Even if the houses are far apart from each other. But it's only a matter of moments before she pulls something metal out from beneath a potted plant, unlocks her door, and ushers me inside.

I have never been in a human-made dwelling before. I didn't realize that humans decorate the inside of their homes. I've garnered enough human speech to understand what some of the things are. Pictures are hung on the walls. Christine seems to love having a plethora of plants surrounding her as well. And she has one entire wall devoted to housing books. I don't know how to read, but I know what books are.

Christine gestures for me to follow her down a hallway. My hooves are loud enough against the wood flooring that my ears pin back against my skull. I attempt to lighten my steps as I follow my human into what I assume is her bedroom. There's a connected room with some kind of reflection wall – a mirror, I think it's called – and a water trough. Oh, that's right. It's called a bathtub.

Christine spins something attached to the wall, and it begins to rain inside the bathtub. She pulls a cloth in front of it. "Okay. I'm going to let the water heat because it takes forever. And then I'm going to shower." She glances away for a moment before meeting my gaze again. "Do you want to shower with me?"

I tilt my head. "I don't normally bathe, love."

She shrugs. "Just thought I'd offer. I have plenty of clean towels and..." Her gaze drops to my feet. "Although it might be a little slick in the tub for your hooves."

She turns to a smaller version of the tub and opens a door beneath it, bending over at the waist. Her pretty, pink pussy is visible as she does, and I find it difficult to keep my cock from extruding. In truth, I've had difficulty keeping it sheathed the entire time I carried her here. Thoughts of how it felt to be inside her are consuming my mind. Why did I say that I don't bathe? For a chance to be intimate with her again, I'd do anything.

I cross my arms, keeping my voice controlled. "On second thought, I would like to shower. I've always wondered why humans fuss so much about it."

She stands up. "Maybe we can put socks on your hooves so you don't slip and fall."

Socks? Oh, she must be referring to foot coverings. "If you think it's necessary."

We spend a minute or so covering my hooves and then I follow her into the shower. I must admit, the hot water is extraordinary against my skin. I've cleansed myself in streams and with cold water that I've gathered, but this is phenomenal. I watch, fascinated, as Christine uses some kind of liquid to cleanse her hair, creating bubbles all over it. The scent is strong and chemical-induced. I much prefer her natural scent, relieved when she rinses it out. Though I will admit, her hair is shinier now.

She places some more in her hand and looks at me. "Do you want me to wash your hair for you?"

I smirk. "I'm too tall for you to reach." As it is, I had to shrink my antlers so I wouldn't destroy her ceiling.

"Hold out your hands then." I do, and she rubs the oily liquid over my palms. "Switch spots with me so you can get your hair wet."

She faces away from me and slides past, her backside brushing my front. Without planning it, I band my arms around her, wiping the liquid over her skin. She freezes at first, tense. I ignore that reaction and lower my face to her shoulder, brushing her wet hair away from the skin with my chin. I kiss her with as much tenderness as I can, my cock extruding a little as I do.

She relaxes against me, tilting her head to the side. I kiss her again, sliding one hand across her breasts, the other down her stomach. "Allow me to cleanse you, mo anam cara." I trace my lips up to her ear, savoring the shudder of her body. "Let me help you relax before we slumber tonight."

Again, she tenses, and my heart speeds up. Why does she react this way? I push down the worrisome thoughts that are clouding my mind and use the oily liquid – soap, I think it's called – to tease her rosy nipples. Her head falls back against me, making it easier to kiss the beautiful column of her throat.

My other hand grazes over her hips to the apex of her thighs. "Part your legs for me, love."

She obeys and I glide my hand over the tuft of hair. I don't think it's possible for me to retract my claws until they disappear. I've never tried. But I was able to use my knuckle to bring her to orgasm before. And if I'm careful, I might be able to use the pad of my thumb. I won't be able to penetrate her with my fingers, but my cock will take care of that.

With careful precision, I press my thumb to her clit. She bucks her hips a little, her mouth falling open. I kiss her shoulder, her neck, her ear, as I stroke her. Her body vibrates against mine, forcing my cock to fully extrude. It rests between her buttocks. I ignore it for now and work on bringing her closer to the edge. Little mewling whimpers are escaping from her. "That's it, love. Such a good girl getting ready to come for me."

Christine moans then as I move my thumb faster against the tiny bud between her legs. My other hand is still teasing her taut nipples. Her chest arches forward as she writhes against me. I didn't even notice that she had brought a hand up behind her to grip my antler, but I do when she wrenches my head a little with the force of her passion. Her other hand is pressed against the wall.

I smirk and nip her neck. "Spread your legs wider for me."

When she complies, I pull my hand away from her cunt. She cries out in frustration but stops as soon as I remove her hand from my antler and place it next to her other hand. "Keep your hands here and brace yourself."

I maneuver her hips and bend down a bit. I have to choke back my groan when my cock enters her tight pussy. She's so wet that I glide in with zero resistance. She moans, resting her forehead against the wall. My thumb resumes its ministrations on her clit while my other hand cups her lovely breast. My hips ram into her again and again, my orgasm getting ready to crash over me as I feel her tighten around me.

My groans are guttural as I move my mouth next to her ear. "You...are...perfect." My hips piston faster against her as her moans increase in volume. "Exquisite."

"Oh god..."

"Beautiful...woman." I nip her earlobe, trying to hold myself back from falling over the edge.

"Cambion!"

My name on her lips, combined with the force of her cunt gripping my cock, sends me spiraling. "Mo anam cara..." I growl as I spill my seed deep inside her. She's panting with the force of my thrusts. I slow my speed, my hands splaying over her lower stomach, as her cunt milks every drop of seed from my cock. I lean my forehead against her shoulder, my breathing heavy.

"Cambion?" Her voice is breathy. "Are you okay?"

"Yes," I whisper against her skin. *No.*

"That was...amazing."

"It was." I kiss her shoulder. *And I am irrevocably undone.*

CHAPTER FIFTEEN

CHRISTINE

I have so many mixed feelings. I didn't intend to let Cambion fuck me in the shower, but goddamn, the male can be so naughty! I've never known a man to pick up on body cues the way he does either. It's almost like he knows exactly what my body needs. Not to mention his words. I get little butterflies in my stomach when I remember what he said to me.

And now we're laying in our favorite position on my bed. Naked because apparently, I don't wear clothes around Deer Boy anymore. The curtains are closed, of course. I'm a little shocked that Rosie, my nosy-as-hell neighbor, didn't barge over and ask me why I was running out of the woods naked. She's always home, but maybe she was busy in her bedroom or something. Either way, I'm relieved that no one came asking questions.

I called Kathleen after our shower and chatted with her while Cambion stood behind me and brushed out my wet hair. She'd been worried sick that I hadn't called her. I told her that my tire got a flat and I spent the night in my car because I didn't want to walk home in the dark and my cell phone had zero service. But everything is good now, and I'll get my tire taken care of tomorrow. She insists on driving me to work. Of course, I agree.

To my utter amazement, Kathleen didn't call my mother. She might worry over me, but she's not one to gossip. And she bought my explanation one hundred percent. Honestly, though, who would believe that I ran into one of the infamous "Not Deer" anyway? Best to leave Cambion out of the picture. I've known Kathleen for years, even though I grew up in Dallas. We met one year in high school when she was on vacation, and we've stayed in touch ever since. It made the most sense to move out here after everything went south with Justin. No better place to start fresh than Bumfuck Nowhere.

Although Kathleen did say something a little disturbing. She told me that Justin called her to ask about me. After grilling her for details, she couldn't tell me much. He called this morning to ask how I was, and he wondered if I'd settled in after leaving him. She's one of the few who knows what happened between my ex and me. I was too ashamed to tell anyone else. And she and I both have a right to be concerned that he's calling her out of the blue, especially since my wallet went missing the same day he called! Maybe I'm just overthinking things. A little voice in the back of my mind warns me that I'm not, but I ignore said voice.

A shift behind me and a gentle press of lips to my shoulder draws me from my thoughts. "What's wrong, mo anam cara?"

There's that weird phrase again. Maybe Deer Boy and the other Forest Demons have their own language. "What makes you think something's wrong?"

A tender caress over my hips. "Your body tensed, and your breathing sped up."

I knew it was a bad idea to invite him to my bed. He can already read me too well. "Just a lot on my mind, I suppose."

When he kisses me behind my ear, I about melt into a puddle. "Speak then. I will listen."

I hesitate, though I don't know why. For fuck's sake, we've been intimate a couple times. Deer Boy helped me make dinner after he finished brushing my hair, something no man has ever done for me. He even shrank his antlers into cute little fawn nubs so he wouldn't wreck my wooden headboard. He's been nothing but sweet and thoughtful despite his haughty, almost narcissistic, words. "Things are...complicated."

"I have a very intelligent mind, mo anam cara. I'm sure I can keep up."

I snort. "Don't forget arrogant."

"Naturally." His breathy chuckle whispers against my neck. "Talk to me, goddess of mine. Perhaps I can bring a different perspective."

His voice is light and teasing, though I sense he really does want to help. I suck in a deep breath. Maybe it would help me to talk about Justin. After all, if the fucker is here in Kentucky? Cambion would be a helpful Being to have on my side. I almost smile with glee at how scared shitless my ex would be if Deer Boy decided to get all protective.

But then my stomach lurches at the thought that he might be here in town. And there is a very good possibility that I am in danger. My chest feels tight and my eyes sting as the inevitable panic sets in. "I'm a little worried about...someone who might be...out to hurt me."

Cambion stills. I hadn't realized his hand was tracing circles on my thigh until he stopped. Without a word, he bands his arm around my stomach and maneuvers his other arm so it's banded around my upper chest. He curls his body around me, entangling his legs with mine. "Breathe, love. Deep breaths."

I suck in a shaky breath, a whimper escaping my lips. "I...*hate* these...anxiety attacks."

"I've got you." He pulls me tighter against him. "I've got you."

I'm not sure how long it takes me to calm down. I focus on the steady sound of his lungs, feeling his chest expand and contract behind me. He doesn't let go or loosen his hold on me. He just holds me until the anxiety passes, and my lungs feel like they're working again. Even then, he keeps his arms banded around me.

When he speaks again, his voice is laced with a growl. "Who is this person?"

Oh boy. If that growl in his voice is any indication, Justin better not make a move against me. In fact, hopefully he's not here at all and my imagination is just running wild. "My ex-boyfriend."

CHAPTER SIXTEEN

CAMBION

I cannot help the possessive snarl that rips from my teeth. "A previous lover is a danger to you?"

Christine moves to roll away from me, putting some space between us. I let her, though I much prefer her cradled against me. My chest squeezes as I think of her panic. I'm already getting the sense that she struggles with irrational fear in the mind. Fear that takes over and keeps her from functioning sometimes. I felt helpless as I held her. I didn't like it. But I won't force her to cuddle me against her will. I don't ever want her to resent me.

She adjusts her pillow and faces me. She takes my hand and plays with it as she begins to speak.

"I was with Justin for a year. Things started off pretty good. He treated me well enough."

My lips curl away from my teeth. "Well enough? What do you mean?"

She traces the lines along my palm, sending tingles shooting up my arm. "He took me out on dates. He bought me flowers. He made sure to call me almost every day. And when I moved in with him after six months, things were going decent."

"Decent." I know she can hear the disbelief in my voice. For a woman to describe a previous lover as "decent", he must've been severely lacking.

"Yes. But once I moved in with him...things got a little weird." She pauses. Though the room is dim, I see her swallow.

My jaw clenches in response, but I hold my tongue. I remind myself that I'm learning to be empathetic. She's vulnerable, and I can still smell the anxiety rolling off her. I reach over and play with a strand of her hair. "Weird how?"

Her fingers move to my inner wrist. "He became more controlling. He didn't, like, keep me in the house or anything. But he wanted to know where I was and when I'd be home. He wanted to know who I was with. He didn't want me hanging out with other guys, and if I did, he would get all pissy and not talk to me for a day or two even though we lived together."

"He ignored you?"

"Yes, or..." Her voice trails off and shame floods her features. I use my fingers to tilt her chin up a little. "Or...?"

Her blue eyes seem glassier all of a sudden. "Let's just say he shamed me for wanting intimacy sometimes."

I blink, confused on multiple levels. Christine's body is delectable. Her curves are perfect, her breasts fit in my hands, and her pussy is beyond words. "What do you mean he shamed you? I don't understand. He didn't find you appealing?"

She looks away from me again. "I don't know. He would make me feel bad for wanting sex every few days. Or he would withhold sex when he was mad at me."

Anger burns through me at the thought of this goddess feeling ashamed of wanting to mate. Now that I've tasted it for myself, I can't imagine going a day without it. And yet this man who supposedly loved her also rejected her. On multiple occasions. "Did he claim to love you?" I spit through my teeth.

"Yes."

I caress her cheek. It feels wet beneath my fingers. Her hurt must be immense if her emotions are leaking from her eyes. "He was not worthy of you, love."

She sniffs and it's all I can do not to take her in my arms again and squeeze her. "I figured that out eventually. But not before he started getting mean. It became normal for him to yell at me over small things. Things that didn't matter. And he started getting weirdly possessive. Telling me that I could never leave him, even while he was treating me as though he didn't love me. It was all so confusing and hurtful." Her voice cracks.

"But you did leave him." I tuck a strand of hair behind her rounded ear. "You came here."

"Yes. Four months ago, I was sitting on my bed, sobbing, while he was at work and I had a day off. I'd tried to initiate sex the night before and he'd pushed me away. And I was so lonely and I hurt all the time, but I was afraid of him too. I didn't know what he was capable of. Weird things have happened around him. People get hurt or go missing, but it can never be traced back to him. I kept thinking, 'What if I go missing?' And so, I packed up a bag before I could talk myself out of it and started driving. I called my best friend out here, and she let me stay with her while she helped me get a place set up."

I wipe her cheeks again. I don't like the way her throat sounds thick, as though she's having trouble speaking. "So why are you concerned about him now?"

Her hand is still tracing gentle circles on my wrist. "He called my best friend this morning to ask about me. I haven't spoken to him since I left. I didn't exactly try to hide from him, but it makes me uncomfortable to think that he might be searching for me."

I have to restrain my monstrous side from exploding out of my body at the thought that this man treated mo anam cara so shamefully. Instead, I shift so Christine is under me. She welcomes me as I kiss her delicate lips with a softness that matches her perfect body. "You listen to me, love." I whisper against her lips. "No man should ever make you feel that you are less than the goddess you are. And no one should ever make you feel unwanted."

She holds my gaze, more tears running from her cheeks as her arms go around me. She buries her face into the crook of my neck and parts her thighs. My cock is already extruding, and I push into her warmth with the gentle tenderness I know she needs from me. I hold her as I make slow love to her, letting her feel just how much she means to me.

Christine kisses my neck as I thrust into her. "Cambion..." Her voice is breathy as her hand slides between us. I shift so there's a bit of space between our hips while still pressing into her with aching slowness. Her fingers tickle my cock as she strokes herself to orgasm. When she comes around me, she whimpers against my neck.

I follow, my forehead pressing to hers as I grunt my release. "You are mo anam cara." I cup her face, using my elbows to hold myself up as I look into her stunning sapphire eyes. "And I adore you."

She doesn't speak as she once again wraps her arms around me, burying her face in my neck. I would be content to stay like this for the rest of my existence.

CHAPTER SEVENTEEN

CHRISTINE

I wake up intertwined with Cambion. And I feel *content*. As a person with a shitty brain, I feel like I *should* be anxious. I'm snuggling with a demon for fuck's sake! A demon who chased me down and almost ate me at our first meeting!

A demon who rescued me from being killed and then healed me. A demon who desires me just as I am. A demon who was so sweet and gentle with me before I fell asleep that it made my chest ache with yearning. My head is pillowed on his chest, my legs tangled up with his. He holds me close, even in sleep. His ear flicks every once in a while. The longer I lie here, the more things I realize I like about him. And yet...he's a demon.

A demon that you welcomed into your body.

So? He was horny. That doesn't mean anything.

Bullshit. You sought his comfort last night like it was oxygen. And he held me through my anxiety attack. He didn't judge me or make me feel less than. He just held onto me.

And yet, I don't know what to feel or think about this situation. I've known him for a little over a day. Two nights. And I've had sex with him three times. In two nights and one day. Partners don't form bonds this quickly, do they? Even Justin and I...

Well, shit. I slept with my ex on the first date. And I basically fell head over heels for him within a couple of days. I guess that's just me. I fall in love fast.

I freeze, anxiety spiking in my stomach and chest. I am *not* in love with Cambion. I can't be. I'm a human woman. He's a Demon Forest Lord. He'll go back to the forest whenever we're done with...whatever this is. I don't even know what to call it. But that's how it always is. I get clingy and the guy leaves. Why is Cambion going to be any different?

You know that's bullshit, too.

Something tells me that Cambion isn't going anywhere. That I'm going to have to push him away if I don't want this. And...would it really be so bad? To let myself fall in love with a male who adores me? *If* he meant what he said. On the one hand, I know my anxiety is sky high right now, but I also find it hard to believe that he understands what he's doing. Yes, he's intelligent. Yes, he has humanity of a sort. But he's never had a relationship of any kind. What if he changes his mind tomorrow? What if he wanders into the forest and never looks back? What if –

A light press of lips to my temple. "My anxious human, what in the world has you so worked up this early in the morning?" Oh god. His voice is all sleepy-sexy.

"Just thinking about...all the stuff I have to do today." I cringe, knowing that's a lie. But I can't tell him what's going on in my head. Something tells me it would crush him.

He's silent, though he kisses my temple again. "I have much to do today as well."

"Oh? And what does a Demon Forest Lord do all day?"

His sexy chuckle vibrates beneath my cheek as a claw-tipped hand glides through the tangles of my hair. "I must circle my territory, making sure all is well with the plants and animals. I must also make sure my land hasn't been trespassed upon by any of the other Forest Lords. If so, I will need to pay them a visit."

I glance over at my bedside clock. I still have an hour until Kathleen shows up. And I don't really want to move from my bed just now. Might as well ask questions to distract myself. "So...why are there Forest Lords anyway? And why do you stay in a small territory rather than wandering the world and exploring?"

"We can go where we please as long as we don't intrude on another Forest Lord's territory aside from just passing through. I have lived many centuries, and have seen much of the world. But until my curse is broken, I will forever be drawn to my circle of territory."

I purse my lips. "Why are you cursed?"

"That's a question I have asked myself many times over the years." He runs a claw through my hair again. "In truth, I cannot say for sure. All I know is that one day, all the Forest Lords were gathered in one place by a powerful Faerie Queen. She was angry with us. Jealous of us, I think. Something about being scorned by one of us. And so, she cursed all seven of us until...well...such a time as we could find the key to breaking our curses."

I don't think I've ever heard him pause to think of wording before. "Do you not want to tell me?"

"It's not relevant."

"But I'm curious." I yelp as he rolls until he's on top of me.

Cambion kisses me with a sort of possessive fierceness, his chest rumbling as his hands grip the sides of my head, his fingers tangling in my hair. I kiss him back because, hot damn! My stomach gets all fluttery, and I want nothing more than to wrap my legs around his waist and let him go to town. But he seems content to kiss me, drawing out each one with slow intensity.

I'd be lying if I said I wasn't wet by the time he rolled off me and stood up. His grin is playful. "You must get ready for work, little human. And I must head into the forest before it grows too late in the day."

I lean up on one elbow, tracing a finger over the pattern in my bedsheets and avoiding his gaze. "Will you be back tonight?"

A hand grasps my chin and forces my gaze up. "And every night for the rest of eternity, mo anam cara." He leans down to kiss me again, his tongue gliding into my mouth with such sensual slowness that my breath catches. "Trust in my word."

Before I can respond, he taps my nose and strides down the hall, his hooves thumping against the wood floor. I hear the back door open and shut. And I'm left to ponder my new reality. If it's even reality...

CHAPTER EIGHTEEN

CAMBION

I lied.

And for the first time in my centuries-long existence, I feel guilty for lying. I haven't had a lot of opportunities to lie, but I've done so on occasion. Usually I lie to humans if they happen to cross my path when my brain is coherent. I tell them everything will be fine.

And then I eat them.

But lying to Christine feels different. And my chest aches as though it's cracking open from the guilt.

I know *exactly* why the Forest Lords were cursed – doomed to hold a monstrous beast inside of us until such a time that we could break our curses and return to our normal selves. Each of us has an individualized curse because the Faerie Queen felt that we all needed to learn our own lessons. My guilt is momentarily assuaged by the anger that ripples through me. How dare some Faerie Queen deign to tell *me* what *I* need? I *know* what I need, which doesn't include her cursing me to force me to work through my issues. I don't care if we exist because of her. It shouldn't give a creator the right to force their creations to change.

Aside from all that, I know how to break my curse. So no, I didn't tell Christine a big lie. But a lie is a lie. A half-truth is a lie. Christine is mo anam cara – my soulmate. The one Being who has the power to break my curse and banish the monster that lurks beneath my skin. And then after three centuries of being labeled a monster, I will once again become a brilliant stag when I shift – restored to a true Forest Lord. The one with a beautiful, stunning rack of antlers. How I have missed my stag. He has become warped and twisted by the curse, and I have no control over when or where I shift.

But I cannot tell Christine that she is mo anam cara. I used the phrase, and I know she didn't comprehend it. I couldn't help myself as the words slipped past my lips to caress her ears. I long to tell her who she is to me. She is questioning herself too much to make me comfortable with divulging that secret, though. It is making my heart feel as though it's splintering down the middle. I cannot hear her thoughts or feel her emotions, but her body language tells me much. She wants me. I can scent her arousal. But I can also scent her fear and anxiety. I've already ascertained that she seems to cycle through anxious thoughts. I fear that some of those are about me, which makes my heart throb even harder.

I also lied about needing to check on the plants and animals. The forest takes care of itself, unless wayward humans overstep that is. But today, I am content to watch Christine from the woods. My eyesight and hearing are far keener than hers. It's easy to watch her get dressed for the day. I have to press my hand to my sheath so my cock doesn't extrude, as aching and hard as it is. It seems my body has developed a craving for my soulmate, and seeing her bare skin makes my skin crawl with the longing to touch her.

I watch and listen as her friend, Kathleen, arrives and enters the house. They discuss nonsense topics before they enter Kathleen's car and drive away. I follow as far as I can – until the forest ends at the edge of the town proper, and there's nothing but houses and shops and businesses along the road. But I watch my Christine's body language through the car window. She is anxious. She is stressed.

Does she worry over me? Does she have second thoughts of being with me? She must know that I will never leave her now. No, I haven't told her she is my soulmate or the power she has over me. But surely, she does not doubt my words? Why should she?

Yet...I am more empathetic than I have ever been. At least, I think I am. I can sense that she is struggling inside her head. She is very fearful, my mate. Which makes me begin to fear that with time away from my side, she will overthink.

Then what will I be left with? I clutch at my chest as I realize I will be forced to live with torn soulmate strings attached to my heart.

CHAPTER NINETEEN

CHRISTINE

Work goes by slower than it's ever gone. I mean, I love working in a bookstore the same as the next bookworm. But today? Not only has business been slower than molasses in the middle of Antarctica – I live in Kentucky. Give me a break on the expressions, okay? – but all I can think about is Cambion, and the expression on his face as he left this morning.

I don't know if it's my gut or my anxiety or what, but I get the feeling he's hiding something from me. What could it possibly be? The horrible, gut-wrenching, catastrophizing reason that comes to mind is that he's using me. He doesn't actually mean the things he's telling me, and he'll get tired of me soon enough. Even the thought of him not coming back to the house tonight? It makes me nauseous. Like so nauseous,

I have to sit down behind the cash register and pretend to organize the junk drawer because I don't feel like I can stand.

What the hell is wrong with me? I'm losing it over a man. Male. Whatever. I don't think it matters at this point. And yet, the more I think about it, the more I'm wondering if it would be better for me to just chalk this whole thing up to a fun fantasy experience and let him go. Tell him that he'd be better off finding some nice female –

Nope. That thought makes me even more sick to my stomach. So now I'm brought to this point. I don't think my little heart can take letting him go. The look in his berry-red eyes when he told me he adored me? Oh my god. I thought only really good actors looked at women that way. Justin certainly never looked at me that way.

I realize I'm crinkling the page of a notepad I'm holding. I smooth it out. You know what? I think I'm just going to take the plunge. I'm already in deep. Sometimes, connections between two souls take years and sometimes they're made overnight. I need to just accept the fact that this connection between Cambion and me formed within a span of hours. My heart is already attached, whether I push him away or not. I'm kind of screwed. Might as well just go for it. Maybe I'll find some happiness for once in my life.

I stand up, my shoulders feeling lighter. Of course, that's how I am. Once I make a decision I've been agonizing over,

I always feel better. Because even if it's the wrong decision, at least I made one. And this decision? I don't think this is one I'll waver on. I'll tell him tonight when he shows up. And if he doesn't show up at my house? Well then. I guess that's my answer. And –

The door chimes open. I have my back to it since I'm now reshelving a couple books that someone decided they didn't want to purchase. "Be with you in just a minute," I say with my bright, customer-service voice. Honestly, it sort of matches my mood now.

"Take your time, sweetheart. I'm in no rush."

I freeze. I would know that voice anywhere. It's the voice that went from sweet to angry within a heartbeat. It's the voice that proclaimed love one moment and then denied it the next. It's the voice that moaned another girl's name while I was giving him a blowjob because he was watching porn instead of being present with me.

I stand up, ignoring the trembling in my stomach, and turn to face him. *Stay calm. Stay cool. Don't let him know you're freaked out as fuck that he's here.* Yeah right. Easier said than done. But I'm very impressed when I manage to speak without my voice wobbling. "What are you doing here?"

Oh god. There he stands in all his human glory. Justin was always the handsome type. He has blue eyes to die for and thick, blond hair that's a dream to run your hands through.

He's tall. He's built. He's sensuous in every way a woman can dream of. But...as I look at him now? All I can see are the things he *doesn't* have.

His lips are full, but not quite as kissable as I prefer. His ears are round, human ears that don't flick at a sound, or perk with an emotion. Though he's built, it's because he goes to the gym, not because he has spent his life honing those muscles from actual use. His eyes are hard. Dead in a way.

He's not my Deer Boy.

I suppose that's another confirmation that I made the right decision.

All of this goes through my head with a moment. It's enough for me to regain my composure.

And in that one moment? His demeanor changes. "I came to see you." His tone is clipped.

I cross my arms over my chest. I'm not brave, but I am far more resolved than I expected myself to be around this man. "You do realize that when I moved to this state that's thousands of miles away, it was because I wanted to end things between us and start fresh, right?"

He mimics my stance and leans against the doorframe of the bookstore with that smirk on his face that tells me he thinks he's God's gift to women. "That's only because you lost your perspective for a minute."

Um...what? "Excuse me?"

"Come on, Chris. You know you miss me."

I raise a brow. "If this is your way of charming me back to you, you're doing a shitty job. I'm not interested."

His smirk grows cold. "What's wrong with you? You never talk this way."

He's right. I don't. But maybe meeting Deer Boy has shifted some core part of me. I still feel the Pavlovian response to cower before Justin. But I remember what Cambion said to me last night.

No man should ever make you feel that you are less than the goddess you are. And no one should ever make you feel unwanted.

It gives me the courage to say what I need to say now. And makes my heart swell at the same time. "Well, perhaps I've changed in the last four months."

"No one changes that fast."

Do I tell him I'm with someone else? An inner warning bell clangs at me. That's only going to infuriate him more. The question is, how do I get rid of him? I could text the shop owner to come in for extra support. She lives down the street, and she's done it before when I've had customers who have been problematic or over my head. But I think that would only infuriate him. I need to end things on my terms, not because someone else forced him to leave. "Regardless, you and I are done, Justin. Most men would take a hint when their ex-girlfriend moves across the country to get away from them."

He stares at me, disbelief on his features. It morphs into desperation. But it's a desperation that seems purposeful. Calculating. Manipulative. "Chris, things aren't the same without you. I'm lonely and I realize that..." He rakes a hand through his blonde hair as he takes a step toward the counter. "I realize that I fucked up, okay? I didn't treat you right. There's a lot that I did wrong and...I'm sorry."

Is he for real right now? I suck in a deep breath, thinking how I can be diplomatic with my wording. "While I appreciate the apology, I think it's best if we part ways. I have no interest in getting back together with you." Had he shown up a week earlier, I might've caved. But now?

Suddenly, I remember my wallet and my overnight bag going missing, and I feel suspicion creep over me. But if he did take them, he probably wouldn't admit it to me. Still... "Hey, Justin?"

Hope shines in his eyes. "Yeah?"

Again, his expression seems manipulative, though I couldn't tell you why. Call it a gut instinct. "Did you...happen to find my car with a flat tire?"

He frowns. There's no hesitation as he responds. "No. Why?"

I shrug. I'm not sure I believe him, but I sure as hell am not going to tell him that. "I was just wondering. Some stuff went missing from it, is all."

He takes another step closer to the counter I stand behind. "Chris –"

"No." I hold up a hand, though my stomach clenches. "I appreciate you coming to check on me, and I really do appreciate the apology. But we're done, Justin. I hope..." I study him, watching as his expression changes to one of sadness. "I hope you have a nice life, okay?"

He just stands there staring at me for a minute. I don't move, ready to text the owner if I need to because at this point, I've said what I needed to say and if he won't leave? I'll have him removed. Then his gaze hardens. "Bye, Christine." And just like that, he's gone.

I watch him get in his fancy Mustang and drive away, his eyes on the road ahead of him. I sag on the stool once he's gone and suck in a shaky breath, my head going to my hands. I take all of six seconds to debate texting Kathleen. My phone rings four seconds after that, and she tells me she's on her way to get me. I call the shop owner and let her know that I'd like to close up early since it's been a slow day and I'm not feeling well, which is true enough. She agrees.

Kathleen doesn't say much when she picks me up, and I don't volunteer information. We take a roundabout way back to my house, and I can't help but notice that she keeps looking in the rearview mirror more often than she normally does.

But I am having an internal freak out now that I'm processing everything that happened. I don't trust him. At all.

We pull up to my driveway twenty minutes later. "Thanks, babe," I murmur as I open the door.

"I should come in with you."

I inwardly laugh at the thought of Kathleen meeting Cambion, even though I have no idea if he's coming back or not. "No, that's okay. I doubt Justin knows where I live. And if he does show up, I'll call the police, okay?" *No need to mention that if Deer Boy sees my ex, the police won't be needed.*

Her hazel eyes narrow in my direction. "Christine Callahan, that psycho drove across several states to 'check on you' and try to get you back. I wouldn't put anything past him."

I shrug, though I do feel uneasy. "I'll be fine, babe. I promise." Kathleen glares at me in disbelief. I know I'm going to have to pull out the big guns at this point without revealing everything. "I, uh, have a guy coming over tonight."

Her eyebrows shoot up into her hairline. "Really?" Then she smirks. "Who is he? Do I know him?"

I rub my forehead. "No comment other than no, you don't know him. I'll see you tomorrow, okay?" I sigh as I remember that my car is *still* sitting a few miles down the road. "I know I need to get my car, but I doubt it's going anywhere tonight. Can we snag it up tomorrow?"

"Sure." She still has that annoying-as-shit smirk on her face.

I pinch my thigh a little to steady myself. "Fine, you nosy bitch. Maybe you can come by and meet him tomorrow night. But I need to make sure he's okay with it first. He's a...private person."

She gives me a knowing grin. "Get some good dick tonight then."

I smack her arm as I get out of the car, smiling at her laughter as she drives away. I turn to face my house. It's early afternoon so it's possible Cambion won't be back for a few hours yet. I unlock the front door and go in, flipping on the kitchen light despite the fact that there's plenty of light from the windows.

I unlock the back door so he can come in and start making dinner so my hands are busy. I tell my Alexa to play my alternative station and focus on the music, humming along. Anything to keep my anxiety from spiraling. I think of my Deer Boy with his kissable lips and soft ears and sensuous hands. I press my thighs together as my core tightens, remembering how good his ridged cock feels inside me. Maybe I don't need music to distract me after all.

It doesn't take long before I hear the door open and close, along with the telltale clomping of hooves across my wood floor. I smile as I continue dicing onions, my stomach doing a little flutter. "Hi, Deer Boy. I hope you like sausage and potatoes."

Warm arms encircle my waist as sharp teeth nip my ear. "Anything you cook will be splendid, little human."

I chuckle and duck away from him so I can get more ingredients out of the fridge. "Anything exciting happen today?" I turn to face him, my breath catching at the heated look in his eyes.

"Not a thing." His voice is a sensuous, baritone caress across my skin, raising goosebumps. "I think the most exciting part of my day was when I repaired a branch that was a little cracked." He stands tall by the counter, one elbow resting on the faux granite.

My mouth goes dry at the sight. He's so breathtaking. Masculine and beautiful in all the right ways. Everything from his soft ears to his strong deer legs. Did I think Justin was handsome? How could I after seeing this perfect male standing before me?

A salacious grin reveals his sharp teeth, his eyes twinkling with mischief. "Something on your mind, love?"

My cheeks feel hot as I turn around. "No, nothing."

His low, rumbling chuckle permeates my bones. "Anything exciting happen to you today?"

"Not exactly. Well, kind of, but not in a good way."

He stills, a predator assessing a threat. "What happened?"

Well shit. Hopefully Justin *doesn't* show up because based on Cambion's tone? He won't leave here alive. "So...remember how I told you I was suspicious that my ex-boyfriend might be here in town?"

CHAPTER TWENTY

CAMBION

M y ears pin to my skull and my lips lift in a silent snarl as I listen to my mate tell me what happened to her today. As far as I'm concerned, that human is dead if he touches her, approaches her, or even breathes in her direction. No one will make my goddess feel uncomfortable. And I mean no one.

"So he didn't threaten me or anything," she finishes as she uses an iron pan to cook the vegetation and meat over the stove.

"He might as well have," I spit between my clenched teeth.

Her cute little nose crinkles as she faces me. "No, he didn't. Not really."

"Why do you sound so unsure then, mo anam cara?"

She doesn't answer me, though I notice the tension filling her body.

I take a step closer to her, protectiveness swelling through me. "It was an unspoken threat. With his body language and his demeanor. He's trying to lay claim to you." And I can't stomach the thought of this insecure human man touching my Christine ever again.

Christine pulls the food off the stove and sets it on a wooden board. She turns to face me, trailing one finger up my chest before laying her palm flat over my heart. "You have no reason to be jealous of him, Cambion."

"Jealous?" Does she misunderstand me so much? I search for any hint of a teasing gleam in her azure eyes. There is none. I cover her hand with mine. "Who said I was jealous, little human?" I widen my grin, making myself look as though I want to devour her. Because I do. I want nothing more than to bury my face in her sweet pussy and feast on her until she gushes on my tongue.

Her eyes darken as she holds my gaze, making my tail flick against my buttocks. She tucks a strand of hair behind one ear and stands on her toes to give me a peck on the cheek. "Come on. It's time to eat dinner."

I swat her firm behind as she walks away from me, smirking at her little squawk of outrage. "If you don't want me touching it, then you shouldn't make it so enticing, little human."

Christine's lips quirk up with mischief as she plates our dinner. I stand behind her, watching her with a little fascination, if I'm being honest. To experience domesticity with my mate isn't something that ever entered my mind. But this feels so normal. A routine, of sorts.

Of course, I haven't forgotten about the human man. Perhaps I need to pay him a visit. He can't be that difficult to track. It's a small town, and my hunch is that he is staying somewhere nearby. Regardless of what Christine says about his benign behavior, I will not rest until I'm certain she's safe.

I follow her to the small table she has and sit down across from her. Sitting in chairs feels strange, I admit. So did sleeping in a bed, but for my mate, I will do it. I can adjust from living in a cave. Though she uses some kind of tool to eat her foot. It irks me that I don't know the names for all the human things she takes for granted. I know I have a keen mind and a somewhat developed vocabulary. But I've never paid attention to what humans call things.

"So..." She spears a potato with her utensil. "I wanted to ask you a question because I'm not sure how this works."

I use my claw to spear my food. "How what works?"

"This thing between us."

This...thing? My ear flicks, giving away my discomfort. I really need to tell her what we are. But I can't do that yet. Not while she's still so uncertain. "In what respect are you speaking?"

She chews for a moment, and I want to flick her pert little nose with my impatience. "Am I allowed to tell people about you?"

This I was not expecting. "Why would you need to?" Because why can we not just live as we are now? I can make my territorial rounds during the day, and she can work in town. Then at night, we will do as we are doing now. It's a perfect routine.

She blinks at me, confusion marring her serene expression. "Well, I want to be able to introduce you to my best friend, for one thing. I know we can't be seen together in my world because it would raise too many questions." I nod as she continues. "But I thought there would be at least a couple of people I might tell."

Oh, I see. She wants those who are close to her to know about me. "Is it a human custom for friends to meet the one you are with?"

"Yes. And it would be...difficult if I couldn't talk about you to my best friend. I tell her everything."

Jealousy flares up in my chest. "Why can you not tell me everything?"

"I never said I couldn't, but I haven't known you that long. I've known Kathleen for years, and I've shared so much with her."

What is this feeling coursing through me? It doesn't feel like jealousy or possessiveness. It feels as though I'm having trouble breathing. It's pain in my heart. Why does my heart hurt?

"Cambion?" Her voice is soft, a touch of fear tinging it. "Why do you look upset?"

I stand up, my claws gouging into the table. I wince, retracting them. "Why can I not be the one you tell everything to? Why do you have to have another who is your best friend? What if I want it to be me?"

"Oh boy." She sighs and gets up, walking around the table. Understanding washes over her features. "I know we aren't done with dinner yet, but come sit with me on the couch for a minute, okay?"

I oblige, letting her lead me to her comfort area. She sits down, patting the cushion next to her. I sit, making sure that my leg is touching hers. She watches me for a moment before climbing into my lap, her knees straddling my hips. My hands move of their own accord to her waist while she winds her arms around my neck. She rests her forehead against mine. I close my eyes, reveling in her scent, her warmth, the comfort of having someone to hold.

Her voice is a breathy whisper when she speaks. "I know you've been alone for a long time, Deer Boy." I smirk at her silly nickname. "But I live in a world where we have friends, family, co-workers, and acquaintances. I need other people in my life too."

A low whine issues from my throat, startling me. What the fuck is wrong with me?

Christine presses a kiss to my cheek. "Just because I care about other people doesn't mean I care about you any less, Cambion. There's room in my heart for you too."

I suck in a breath. Is she saying what I think she's saying?

She cups my face in her hands as she kisses the tip of my nose. "I really want you to meet Kathleen. She, of all people, won't judge me for being with you. And she'll want to meet you once I mention you. Trust me. She might even lecture you about breaking my heart."

I move my lips to the palm of her hand, kissing it. "I don't think you understand. I could never break your heart, Christine. Never."

She holds her breath as I kiss her hand again, nipping at her finger. "Why...is that...Cambion?"

I hold her gaze, feeling as though it's the most natural thing in the world. "You are mo anam cara. We are bound together for eternity."

"You keep saying that phrase but...you've never said the word 'eternity' with it. What...what do you mean?"

Her hands slide to my shoulders with a calm the rest of her body isn't experiencing. I can hear her heart pounding beneath her ribs. I mimic her from a moment ago and cup her face in my hands. "You are my soulmate. My fated one." Even I can hear the adoration and affection in my tone.

Christine's fingers fidget against my shoulders. I'm learning this is a response to her anxiety that she tries to hide.

I brush my thumbs over her round cheek. "It's okay, love. You don't need to do anything different. The only reason I'm telling you this is because I want you to understand that I will never break your heart. I will never want another. You are the one who is fated for me." I hope she can hear the truth ringing in my voice because I mean every word.

She holds my gaze, her fingers still moving along my shoulders. But after a moment, she slides them into my hair. "Is...that a promise? Because earlier today, I was feeling really weird about how close we've gotten in such a short time. I've never believed in the whole soulmate thing. But I guess if it's true, it makes sense."

I brush a light kiss to her lips. "It's a promise. You are doing nothing wrong by being with me. Our souls call to each other."

"What if..." She sucks in a deep breath. "What if I'm not sure? What if I need time to...to think about this?"

My heart is the one pounding now. "There are strings connecting my heart to yours. I feel them." I swallow. *Why does this hurt me to say?* "If you choose to walk away from me, I will let you. I am a Forest Demon, but I'm not a monster." She flinches, perhaps remembering she called me such. "I would never force you to be with me, but if you reject," my breath catches, "reject me, I will forever feel this unfulfilled bond."

She fiddles with my hair. This is a good thing, I tell myself. She is not running away or trying to put space between us. Vulnerability is not something I'm used to. Maybe I will never get used to it. But the moment felt right to tell her. After making me wait far longer than I'm comfortable with, she sucks in a tremulous breath. "So we can continue what we're doing now? I don't have to do some weird ritual or something?"

I chuckle, relief coursing through me, though her words bring a bit of sadness to mind. "No. No weird, demonic ritual. I am content to be with you as we are now." Of course, then my curse will never be broken. But would it be so bad? As long as I get to be with Christine, I can live with the monster that prowls beneath my skin. And if I tell her that there is, in fact, a ritual to break my curse, she may want to complete it. And I...don't know if I can live for what it calls for.

Her hands move to my antlers, tracing them. They aren't sensitive in the way my ears and cock are, but I feel what she's doing. And just the act of her straddling me, touching me, has made me ache with need.

As if she can tell, she kisses me, her tongue delving between my lips. I groan and kiss her back, gripping her hard enough that I worry my claws will cut her. I let out a growl when she stands up, but cut myself off when I watch her shuck off her pants and toss them to the side. My cock extrudes at the sight. She smirks as she makes a show of pulling her shirt off as well.

I crook my finger at her. "Come here and sit on my lap like a good girl."

Her eyes darken as she obeys, sauntering the three steps over to me. I yank her on my lap and impale her with my shaft. She gasps, but I know she was ready. I can smell the arousal leaking from her, and her inner thighs are slick with her need. Her fingers clutch my shoulders as I grip her hips and pick her up, slamming her back down on me. I thrust upward at the same time, finding a rhythm.

She gasps and moans, her beautiful breasts bouncing as I thrust into her over and over. My tongue darts out of its own accord and licks across the taut, rosy bud of her nipple. I can't risk cutting her with my claws, so I slow my thrusts enough to guide her hand to her wet cunt. I lean forward and growl in her ear. "Make yourself come so I can hear you scream my name."

She shivers, her fingers teasing her clit in rounded, fast strokes. I buck into her over and over, slamming her down on my cock harder and harder.

"Oh god. Oh fuck. Cambion!" Her cry is loud in my ears as her cunt squeezes me like a fist.

I kiss her hard enough to bruise and thrust into her a few more times before my release throws me over the edge. I almost see stars, I come so hard. Remembering to shrink my antlers, I rest my forehead on her shoulder as she wraps both arms around me, pressing her face to the crook of my neck.

"My heart," I whisper against her skin.

Her response is to kiss my neck and hold me tighter. No male could ever be more content than me in this moment.

CHAPTER TWENTY-ONE

CHRISTINE

A full-on migraine is what I awake to the next morning. Though I would otherwise be content to keep myself intertwined with Cambion, my head pillowed on his chest, I roll over with a groan and cover my face with my blanket.

Two seconds later, his hand is on my side. "Love? Is something wrong?"

"Head. Hurts," I mumble into my pillow.

His hand glides to my back, where he soothes me with long, languid strokes. "Why does your head hurt, little human?"

Ugh. I so do not want to explain what a migraine is while I have one. "I get bad headaches called migraines. Sometimes they're brought on by stress. Other times, I just get them. I'm not sure why I woke up with one today."

He glides his claws through the tangles of my hair, making my scalp tingle. "What can I do to help you?"

I sigh at the contact. Though it doesn't help my head, it's still soothing. "I have pills in my mirror cabinet in the bathroom. If I take some with a glass of water, it usually goes away in a couple of hours."

The bed shifts and then I hear his hooves on the rug as he goes into the bathroom. A pause and then, "Which pill bottle is it?"

I tell him the name and am met with silence. Oh shit, he probably can't read. "It's the little orange bottle with the white cap. There should only be one bottle like it." No sense in shaming him for something that isn't his fault. Maybe that's something I can teach him in the near future. Not today though. I press against my temple as another throb wracks my inner skull.

Cambion's hooves clomp down the hallway to the kitchen, where I hear him grab a glass and fill it with ice and water from the fridge. I also hear him putzing around in there for a few minutes, opening cupboards and such. I don't even have the wherewithal to care what the fuck he's doing. Hopefully he didn't get distracted and forget to bring me my medicine.

His hooves clomp back down the hall toward me, making me wince. He sets something down on my bedside table and then even through the blanket, I can tell my room is getting more dim. I peel back the blanket to see a tray near me. There's a glass of orange juice, another glass with the ice water, a couple slices of bread, and an orange. The correct pill bottle is sitting next to the orange juice.

Claw tips brush the hair away from my eyes. "Do you need anything else, love?"

I shake my head and sit up, making an effort for him since he's being so damn sweet. I take a couple of pills, and then nibble on the bread and sip the orange juice. "Thank you, Deer Boy."

He grins as he tucks my hair behind my ear, his claws trailing along my jaw. If I didn't feel like shit, I'd want to jump his bones right now. "I was going to make my territory rounds, but I can stay if you need me to."

I wave him off. "No, I'm just going to nap off my migraine. I'll call my boss and let her know I'm not coming in today. Oh shit! Kathleen will be here soon, won't she?" I grab for my phone, dropping it on the floor in the process.

Cambion chuckles and picks it up, handing it to me.

"Thank you." I wince when I check the time. "She'll be here in twenty minutes. Crap. I need to call her first."

He leans down and presses a kiss to my forehead. "I will be back this afternoon. Take care of yourself, love." With that, he strides down the hallway. The back door opens and shuts.

I feel hollow inside now that he's gone. I shouldn't. I know he's coming back. Maybe I should've asked him to stay. Hell, with what he declared last night...

Holy. Shit. Soulmates? Fucking soulmates?

Why should anything surprise me at this point, though? I've already gone over and over this in my mind. My reality paradigm shifted irreparably a couple days ago, and it's not going back to the way it was. Why not throw soulmates into the mix? Hell, maybe I can become a Forest Lord too. Lorddess? Is that even a word? No, I'd be a Forest Lady. Ugh. This stupid ass migraine is making me all woozy and fuzzy.

I finish the food he brought and lie down, closing my eyes. What a thoughtful little Deer Boy. He brought me easy-to-eat food. He closed the blinds so it wasn't so bright. The quiet of my house is welcome. Shit! I need to call Kathleen!

I catch her when she's already on the way over, but she says it's no biggie. She has to pass my house on the way to her work anyway. I wave off her offer to get me fast food and promise her we'll get together soon. Tonight doesn't seem like a good idea, especially considering the conversation Cambion and I had about me having other friends. That's going to have to be addressed, and soon. I get off the phone with my bestie and then call my boss. She assures me it's no big deal and she'll see me tomorrow. I have a momentary anxious moment that she might fire me, but she's almost like a second grandma to me. I'll get her a thank you gift for being so understanding.

I plug my phone back in and lay down. I think about getting up and locking the back door because I don't think Cambion knows how. Then I laugh at myself. My still-unlocked car is sitting down the road a few miles. Since when do I care about locking the door to anything? No one is going to bother me.

Of course, then my mind fixates on my unlocked door for the entirety of my fitful nap. I think I doze on and off. Time doesn't seem to be passing at all, but when I check my phone, I see that three hours have gone by. Huh. Guess I did manage to fall asleep. And my head feels better, thank God. There's still a dull ache in my temples, but it's gone into the background enough that I can sit up without complaint.

I finish the tepid glass of orange juice and get up, taking my tray to the kitchen. I decide I need to brush my teeth and take a shower because my thighs are sticky with demon cum. I smirk. That sounds so dirty to me. Honestly, I can't imagine my life without Cambion in it now. As I shower, though, my thoughts stray more toward the guilt-filled rather than the content.

Cambion declared himself to me last night. Even if he didn't say the phrase "I love you", he still told me, in no uncertain terms, that he was by my side until I send him away. And while I straddled his lap, he'd whispered, "My heart." I didn't miss the tremble of his strong, sure body beneath my hands. I also didn't fail to note the way his heart was pounding in his chest, and I'm pretty sure it was more than the exertion of sex that was making it pump so hard.

I'm learning that my Deer Boy isn't used to being vulnerable. I'm guessing there's more going on beneath the surface than he's telling me. He comes across as arrogant, maybe a tad narcissistic. But his actions are far from that as we spend more time together. He's giving in a way I've never experienced. He's thoughtful and sweet. He's tender and gentle when he needs to be. And it's clear to me now that he is head over heels for me. I can't doubt the sincerity of his words – not when he told me we are soulmates, nor when he's declared his feelings.

Cambion loves me.

The question is...do I love him?

I snort as I shut off the shower and towel myself off. Is it even a question I have to ask? Because even if I can't say the words, I know the answer.

Okay, so our relationship won't be traditional. We can't go out on dates or stroll down the street, hand in hand, without people asking some serious questions. But do I really need that? We can create date nights right here in my house. We can stream the latest movies from my TV instead of going to the theater. Once I get my car taken care of, we can drive anywhere we want. Visit other states. Do we need to abide by societal norms to be happy?

As I get dressed and think over what my life will be like with him, I honestly don't feel like I'll be missing out on much. And once I establish needed boundaries regarding friendships with other people, I'll still be able to hang out with them. Go on vacations. I mean, honestly? I can see myself living with Deer Boy long term.

My hand flies to my belly when I think of the fact that I've had non-condom sex with Deer Boy. Many times at this point. I doubt I have to worry about disease. And I remind myself that I have an IUD inserted. But...is there a possibility for more than just me and him? Can we have children and raise a family together? Part of me hopes we're compatible in that way, even though I'm not ready for a family right now. Fantasy romance novels aren't exactly an accurate guide to whether or not such a thing is possible. But that's a conversation for a much, *much* later time.

For all intents and purposes, I'm already all in. I know it. Deep down, I think I *have* known it since the first time I had sex with him. I just haven't admitted it aloud. And that's what has me feeling guilty. He deserves to know that I want him. I love him. He's my heart too, and we'll discover what life has to offer us as a mated pair.

I snort as I brush out my wet hair. That sounds so weird...but right, too. He says I'm his soulmate. I don't feel some weird bond between us. There's nothing that I can tug on like the books say. But I do feel connected to him. In more ways than one. I don't think I need anything else to confirm what I just admitted to myself. And as soon as he returns tonight, I'll tell him. Because there's no doubt in my head that he'll come back. I know he will.

I head to the kitchen, my bare feet sticking to the wood floor a bit since they're still damp, and start making myself some lunch. I really do need to get my car figured out. I'll text Kathleen and ask her to meet me here after work. We can use her spare tire so I can get it to the shop downtown. Of course, I'll need an appointment, because "small town". But that's –

Something presses to the back of my head. I freeze, my body locking up. Breaths against my neck raise goosebumps on my arms.

"We need to have a little chat, you and me."

I try to breathe. I really do. But if anything is going to spike my anxiety, it's this. "What is this? What are you doing?"

My neck bends forward with the force of the metal object being pressed against my skull. My lungs squeeze shut at the next snarled phrase out of his mouth. "First, you're going to tell me why I saw you fucking some kind of animalistic monster."

CHAPTER TWENTY-TWO

CAMBION

I can't stop thinking about her. Even as I stalk my territory, all I can focus on is her soft, exquisite body beneath mine. On top of mine. In my lap. All the ways I've had my mate, and all the ways I intend to claim her. Maybe I shouldn't have left her, hurting the way that she was. I don't like to see her in pain. But she said she would be fine once she slept. And I know that if I'd stayed with her, I wouldn't have let her sleep.

Even now, I'm desperate to be buried inside her again. I let out a derisive snort as I finish the loop and make my way toward her house. Perhaps I've developed an addiction. I didn't know it was possible to become addicted to a person. I'm a little familiar with the concept of addiction to substances, though I wouldn't know what that's like. But if it's comparable to what I'm experiencing in this moment, I pity anyone who struggles with it.

Christine is essential to my existence at this point. Her questions last night were to be expected. I know that. But the thought of her sending me away from her side? My staggering steps falter a bit, my hand going to my chest, my claws digging into my skin, though not deep enough to cut. I'd respect her wish, yes. But I'd always be in the shadows, lurking, watching, unable to leave her in good faith. I'd stalk her like the shameless beast I am, hungering for her, living the rest of my existence on a hope that she might ask me back to her side.

I still haven't told her about everything that entails our bond. There's no rush. I doubt she'll feel betrayed when I do tell her. But instinct warns me that she's not ready for all the information yet. Her human mind can only process so much information at once, and I know she's had significant change in the last two days. Everything she once believed to be true is shifting to a new outlook, and she needs time to adjust to each piece of knowledge. I will protect every part of her, even if she angers because I'm withholding things. I will explain my reasoning and she will take it in stride as I've observed from her so far.

I smile. My human is resilient if nothing else. But there is so much more to her. She's beautiful, brave, attentive to my needs, soft, kind, affectionate. The ache of loneliness that I ignored for so long is waning. I feel as though I can breathe to my full capacity now. My hooves bound in longer strides, eating up the distance to her home. I want to be with her again. I want to hear her glorious laugh. I want to watch the light reflect off her hair as she walks. I want to stand behind her while she cooks, distracting her with teasing touches. I want –

My thoughts draw up short as I reach the edge of the woods. Her house is in view, but something is different. There is another scent that does not belong. There is a clearing of grass that separates me from the house, but even from this distance, I can smell that another human has been here, near where I'm standing now. The windows are easy to see through. I can see the back of the couch where Christine straddled my hips last night.

My nostrils flare as the monster within threatens to burst from my skin. The human scent mixing with hers is male. And I'm both angered and terrified that another male is here with her. I haven't forgotten that her previous lover visited her yesterday. If the words she spoke are true, he gave an unvoiced threat to her. And I will not tolerate *anyone* threatening my mate. I will rip out his throat if he's hurt her or entered her house uninvited.

What if she invited him in?

That thought draws me up short. What if she tires of me and wants to return to him? To welcome him back into her arms? The thought makes my chest so tight that a whine escapes my lips. The idea that she might willingly let another male touch her, caress her...

I am bound to her for the rest of my existence. I will never be able to leave her side without feeling excruciating pain. So I would be forced to watch or listen as she made her little cries of pleasure with another male. I would –

I shake my head. Her scent was tinged with anxiety when she spoke of the other man. Justin. She would not be a willing participant to any advance he made. Which means he would be forcing her. I swallow the roar from my throat as I charge to the back door of the house, my hooves gouging the grass. I care not who sees me. No one will harm my mate. And I have not eaten human flesh in a few days. I will consume this male and I'll do it gladly.

I fling open the door, slamming it shut behind me. "Christine?"

There is no answer, though I hear the sound of anxiety-riddled breathing coming from her bedroom. Is my mate in a panic? Further proof the male intruder is not welcome. I stride down the hallway, murderous rage fueling my steps. If he's done anything to my mate, I will rip his limbs from his body before twisting his skull from his spine.

Her bedroom door is closed partway. I storm through, the door slamming against the wall with enough force that I'm surprised it didn't splinter. Christine stands in the middle of the room, her blue eyes unreadable. Whatever panicked breathing I heard before, I don't hear it now. She seems both tense and calm. Her hands are clenched into fists at her sides. The scent of the other man is strong, as though he was just here.

Whatever anger I feel cools when I see that she is alone. I cross the room in two strides, my hands going to her shoulders. "Love, are you well?"

She doesn't move. If anything, she tenses under my touch.

Something aches beneath my ribs, but I ignore it, sliding my hands down her arms. "What is it, love? What's wrong?" Something is amiss here. I don't know what it is, but I intend to find out. "Did he come for you? Did he hurt you?"

Christine closes her eyes for a moment, her body giving one violent shiver. I move to envelop her in my arms, but she places a hand on my chest and pushes me. Hard.

I stagger back, disbelief coursing through me. She isn't strong enough to move me, but the force of her rejection is. The ache beneath my ribcage grows heavier. "Christine?"

"Don't touch me."

I flinch at the venom and disgust in her voice. My ears pin to my skull as my tail tucks against my body. "My mate –"

"You are no such thing to me." Her eyes blaze with anger, and yet they are glassy, as though filling with tears.

The ache is a roaring pain now. My chest feels as it did the time I got into a territorial fight with the Fox Forest Lord and he cracked two of my ribs. No, I take that back. It pains me far more than that did. "I don't understand." A low whine follows my words. "You are my heart."

My mate turns her face away, closing her eyes. Tears stream down her cheeks. She swallows once, twice. Her throat is thick when she speaks words that send a fissure down the center of my chest. "I don't want you. Leave me alone. Forever."

I stumble backward again with the force of those words, as though her weak, human body dealt me a death blow. My eyes sting as my vision blurs. "I..." But I have no words. I feel as though I am breaking, splintering apart, shattering. I hunch over, caving in on myself.

Christine turns her back to me, her head bowed. "Leave my house. Never return."

I back out of the room, stumbling as though I've consumed fermented mushrooms. I fling myself down the hall on unsteady legs, the heartstrings connecting me to my mate squeezing with fierce intensity. I ignore the pull to stay with her as I crash through the door and bound into the woods. My form breaks as I run through the trees, my face becoming furred and my snout lengthening to that of a deer. My claws extend and rip through trunks as I go, heedless of the damage I am doing to my territory.

The heartstrings squeeze me tighter, as though pleading with me to return. But I cannot. I cannot ignore the wish of my mate, even if it torments me until I am nothing but a raging wraith of pain crashing through the forest.

CHAPTER TWENTY-THREE

CHRISTINE

A sob rips from between my teeth as I fall to my knees, my head in my hands. I'm shaking so hard my teeth are clacking together. I will *never* forgive myself for being responsible for the devastating hurt in Cambion's eyes as I delivered those words. Flung them at him. Hurt him more deeply than I've ever hurt anyone. If I ever doubted the truth of the soulmate connection we have, that just sealed it for me.

And now I've lost him. But at least he's safe. Because in the conversation we had before I fell asleep in his arms last night, he told me he can be killed despite the fact that he's immortal. Not by another Forest Lord. But things can kill him. We didn't get into specifics. But the only phrase repeating in my head right now is *Deer Boy can be killed. Deer Boy can be killed.*

A hand grips my shoulder, yanking me to my feet. "Get up." Justin sneers at me, his right hand holding the gun so it's pointed toward the floor. "That was quite the performance."

If he didn't have a weapon in his hand, I would slap him hard enough to make his teeth sink into his cheek. "Fuck you," I spit. Probably not my wisest move, but tears are still streaming down my face. "So what now? I did what you asked. But to what end? Why force me to break the heart of the male I love, huh? What purpose does that serve?"

Justin's eyes grow cold. Dead. "Love?"

I swipe at my wet cheeks. "Yes. Love. I love him. And you just forced me to break his heart. Why? What do you have to gain from this endeavor? What?" I'm shouting now.

Despite his dead eyes, he smirks. "Now, I get you back."

I stare at him in disbelief. "You think I'll get back with you after what you've just done?"

Justin's eyes gleam in an unnatural way. I can't even describe it. It's almost like he's been gripped by a bout of insanity. "I think you'll come back home with me since you know what I'm capable of now. You won't dare leave me again, will you? Now that you know I'll always come for you."

Is this real? Can this be my reality right now? "You didn't even like me much towards the end of our relationship!" My heart pounds so hard and so fast, I worry I might fall straight into a panic attack. "You weren't attracted to me, as you stated multiple times. You were mean. Cruel even. Why do you want me back?"

"Is that what you think?" His voice is tinged with desperation. "You think I didn't want you? Christine, I was crazy jealous! You must be remembering things wrong." He steps closer, grabbing my shoulder with the hand doesn't hold the gun. "You were close with your friends, especially Tony. And I was so afraid of losing you. But I couldn't help my behavior. You were making me insane." He grips my shoulder tight enough to bruise.

The man is clearly delusional. I still don't know what the hell game he's playing. I know I'm not crazy. I know how he treated me. What's his end game, though? I don't understand. I do know that I need to get the upper hand somehow. But what can I do? An insane thought crosses my mind, but it might be worth a shot. Ugh, the thought of what I'm about to do makes me sick. But I'm running out of options, here.

I place a hand on his chest. "You were jealous?"

Thank God he releases my shoulder. He covers my hand with his, caressing the skin with his thumb. "And terrified of losing you."

My skin is crawling, even as his words don't ring true. They remind me of poorly delivered lines by a stage actor who's done the show one too many times. Like he's memorized something and now that he's performing, the scene isn't quite playing out like he thought it would. But I have to continue my role. "You didn't lose me."

"I know." A smirk crosses his face, his hand gripping mine even as the gun in his other hand bangs against my hip. "I'll never lose you because I'll always come after you. See." He closes the short distance between us, our chests almost touching. My skin prickles with a sense of wrongness. "My last girlfriend didn't understand that no one gets to walk away from me. And I mean no one. She paid the price that you will pay if you don't come home with me."

Holy. Shit. Dread slicks down my spine at the implication. "You told me Melody died in a car accident."

His eyes narrow a bit. "Oh, did I?"

Keep him talking. Keep him talking. "What happened then?"

Justin brushes some hair off my shoulder. "A month before I met you, she tried to leave. She even moved out, just like you did. But I tracked her down. And when she wouldn't come back with me..." He shrugs, a maniacal grin spreading his lips.

"You're insane," I breathe.

"I will not be abandoned the way my mother abandoned me!" Justin lets go of me, turns, and slams his fist down on my dresser.

And I've had enough. I tackle him now that he's off balance. We sprawl to the floor, the gun spinning across the rug. I landed on top of him and now I'm scrambling to get off. I throw myself toward the gun and grab it. Justin reaches for my ankle, but I kick out, managing to hit his face.

I have about one point five seconds to figure out my next move. I know that when you aim a gun at someone, you have to be ready to shoot them. And even though I hate Justin more than I've ever hated anyone in my entire life, I don't know if I can kill another human being. Then again, who will believe me? Justin has talked his way out of murder before, maybe more than once. I vaguely recall him mentioning that his mother disappeared, and the police were never able to find her. How did I never put the pieces together?

I point the gun at the well-dressed sociopath, my finger on the trigger. "Don't even come at me, or I will shoot you."

Justin stands, keeping his hands raised. "You don't know how to use a gun, darling. Give it to me." He takes a step toward me.

I shoot him in the thigh. I was actually aiming for his kneecap, but I wasn't expecting the kickback from the pistol. He screams, clutching his leg as he falls to the ground. I shoot him again, my aim a little off-center of his stomach. He groans, his blood beginning to pool on my rug. I keep the gun pointed toward him, but he stills. I don't even think he's breathing anymore.

I'm also not one of those idiots that bends over the body when the villain is supposedly dead. The last thing I need is for him to grab me or grab the gun. I back away from him, keeping the gun trained toward his prone form. I shut my bedroom door and then sprint down the hall, keeping the gun gripped in my hand. I slide my feet into my sneakers and run out the back door.

It doesn't take me long to find Cambion's trail. It seems he's destroying the trees as he goes. He must be in his monstrous form. I flee into the woods, hoping and praying I'm not too late and that when he sees me, he won't go into a rampage and try to kill me.

I have to right my wrong and fix this. I have to mend his poor, wounded heart and tell him the words I should've said last night. I have to apologize for letting Justin scare me enough that I went along with his scenario. I should've told Cambion the truth, but Justin threatened to shoot Cambion on sight if I didn't play a role to get rid of him. I panicked. But we'll take care of Justin soon enough. First things first.

I can't lose my Deer Boy. I'll do whatever it takes to repair the damage I've done.

Because I love him.

CHAPTER TWENTY-FOUR

CAMBION

In my rage-fueled mad dash, I must have circled back around until I was close to Christine's house again. Ever since I recognized my soulmate, the monster has not turned my mind into a puddle of goo. I'm still very conscious of my actions, even while I've been running through the forest. I was not paying attention to direction though.

Perhaps my heartstrings have more influence over me than I thought because I can see the outline of her house through the trees.

But then I hear the distinct sound of a gun. I skid to a halt, the fur and snout on my face sinking back beneath my skin. My heart hammers for a different reason now. The gunshot was muffled, as though it came from inside a building.

A second shot rings out.

Silence.

There are only a few handfuls of bounds that separate me from my mate's home. I hear clearly when a door slams against the side of the house and footsteps pound across the grass. My body moves of its own accord as I recognize the cadence of those steps. Right now, I don't care what words came out of her mouth. I will think of them later. If the sound of guns came from her house, the other man was there. And if she runs now…

I will protect my mate, even if she doesn't want me. I will never let her fight for her life alone. I sprint toward her form as it streaks in my direction. I can tell the minute she spots me. A sob rips from her mouth as she closes the distance toward me, her arms outstretched. I don't even chide her when I open my arms, accepting her as she slams into me.

I stagger back a little with the force of her momentum, but I am strong. My arms wrap around her as she sobs against my chest. Something metal digs into my back for a moment before it falls to the ground behind me. My own eyes sting as I wrap my arms around her, holding her to me. I feel an echo of rejection, but I ignore the tearing pain in my chest. My mate needs me right now. I will deal with the upcoming separation when it happens.

I try to pull away enough that I can look at her, but she clings to me, still sobbing against my chest. Incoherent words burble from her lips, but I can make out two of them. "I'm sorry."

I don't smell blood on her. I don't think she's injured since she was running fast. My initial fear of her harm is morphing into anger at her earlier cruel words. I grip her a little more forcefully and pull her away. My lips are curled in a snarl, even as my eyes continue to burn. My heart throbs inside my chest as I meet her tear-filled gaze. "Why?"

I haven't shouted, but she flinches anyway. "I had to."

She reaches for my face, but now that the initial fear of her injury has worn off, I have little room for anything but rejection and pain. I flinch away.

"Cambion, please." Desperation coats her words. "I had to."

My heart softens at the pleading on her face. "What do you mean you had to?"

She gestures to the piece of metal that fell behind me. Perhaps the gun I heard? "He saw you running toward the house and told me that if I didn't make you go away, he would kill you." She wrings her hands. "I had seconds to decide, and I couldn't risk you. Cambion, I –"

She lied to me. To protect me. My lips cover hers even as one hand slides into her hair, the other cupping the back of her neck. The hurt within my chest is still there, but it's giving way to the realization that I should have followed my instinct.

I knew the man had been there. I let my own pain get in the way of seeing the truth. I push her backwards, still kissing her, until she's pressed against a tree.

Her lips meet mine with fervor, her arms winding around my neck. I groan low in my throat as she slides her hands up through my hair. She pulls away enough to whisper against my lips. "Forgive me. I'm so sorry."

I graze my nose against hers. "There's nothing to forgive." Even now, I feel that the gaping hole in my chest is filled. I am whole once more. "I should've paid more attention. I'm just glad you aren't hurt."

Her lips tremble as her blue eyes fill with tears again. "I had to shoot him, but I don't think he's dead. We need to –"

I press a finger to her lips as I kiss her cheek. "We'll deal with it in a moment. Don't worry now, love. You're here with me again. You're safe."

She closes her eyes. "You aren't mad at me? You still love me?"

I cage her in a little more, one hand going to either side of her head, my claws digging into the bark of the tree. "Look at me." I wait for her to open her eyes. I have more words to say, but the emotional depths I see stun me to silence. I kiss her with a low groan, pressing my body to hers. My fingers are in her hair, my tongue slicking into her mouth.

She moans in her throat, giving back everything I'm throwing at her. Our kisses are hard enough to bruise, but it seems neither of us cares. I can't get enough of her taste, her scent, the soft pliancy of her curves against me. I thought I'd lost her. I thought she was forcing me from her side because she didn't want me. I thought I'd never feel the warmth of her in my arms again.

My hands glide down her body. I savor the globes of her breasts for a moment, teasing her nipples through her shirt and drawing out a groan, before moving to her hips and thighs. I hoist her up, my hands gripping the underside of her thighs. Her legs wrap around my waist, trusting me to hold her.

I break the kiss for a moment, pressing my forehead to hers. "I love you, my goddess. Nothing you ever do will make me stop loving you. You are my heart."

She whimpers and kisses me again. "Cambion, I –"

The crack of a twig and rustle of leaves sounds from behind me. My ear flicks even as I move with lightning speed, maneuvering Christine so she's on her feet and shielded by my body. Full awareness comes upon me as I watch a man pick up the gun from the ground. He's hunched over, covered in blood, and shaking like a leaf in the wind. But he has the gun trained on me. Despite his white pallor, he's strong enough to shoot me. The barrel of the gun points right at my chest.

I crouch an inch, though I know he can fire the gun before I can reach him. But I'm fast enough to end his life before the bullet completes its damage and I sprawl on the ground. I told Christine true last night. Though immortal, I can die. And I'm certain a bullet is one of the things that can kill me. But I will take him down before he kills me.

He sneers as he squeezes the trigger, and I prepare to dart toward him. I'll be able to snap his neck before –

A blur of movement in front of me. A yelping, feminine cry. A tangle of limbs as the body of my mate is thrown backward against me, a red stain spreading across her chest a moment later. I catch her instinctively, my eyes wide, my ears pinning back against my skull.

The man stumbles back a step, his face a mixture of surprise and pain, as though he wishes he could take the last few moments back. The gun drops from his hand as he slumps over, dropping to one knee. "Foolish girl," he rasps. "Dammit. Dammit." He holds his head in his hands. "I didn't mean to kill this one. I didn't. I didn't."

I ignore the man's pleading words and kneel down, my beautiful, precious mate in my arms. My mate, who is bleeding out from a wound in her chest. My mate, whose heart is slowing even now. My mate, who is looking at me with an unspoken emotion that makes my heart squeeze. I press my forehead to hers. A strange keening is coming from me as I hold her against me, willing her to stay with me.

"Cambion."

Her weak voice penetrates my cries, though my vision is too blurry to make out her features. I huff a sob. I'm...crying? I've never cried before today. Even when I thought Christine rejected me, I was merely teary-eyed and broken. I didn't sob as I am now. But I feel as though I'm shattering from the inside out. "Why?" I manage to choke out.

Her blood is slowing in her body. Her heart is pumping with a sluggishness that belies my wishes for her to live, the telltale sign of what's coming. Her trembling hand cups my face, her thumb brushing my wet cheek. "I love...you."

Another sob wracks my chest.

"I...love you, Deer...Boy."

"Mate."

Thu-thump. Pause. *Thu-thump.*

"Mate, no."

Thu-thump. Thu...

"Mate...please..."

There is no answer to my desperate plea. My mate is gone.

CHAPTER TWENTY-FIVE

CHRISTINE

Is death supposed to be so damn uncomfortable?

Because I see no light at the end of the tunnel, that's for sure. There isn't even a tunnel. I'm stuck in some kind of weird paralysis state. I can't move my body. There's a sense of impending doom. I hear the whine of my broken-hearted mate as he begs me not to die. And then, it's almost like I'm ripped from my body, but the sensation isn't painful.

One second, I'm stuck, unable to move. The next, I'm looking down at my body. I guess I'm floating above it? I'm watching Cambion cradle my body, tears still streaming down his face. Even though I'm a spirit or a ghost or whatever, my heart is breaking into tiny little pieces for him. The devastation on his face is gut wrenching, and I want nothing more than to hug him to me. Did I truly believe him to be a monster when I first met him? Because the depth of emotion I see pouring from him... If only it was enough to bring me back to him.

I watch as he sets me on the ground, his claws brushing my hair behind my ears. His chest is heaving, his cheeks wet and shining. A strange whining whimper keeps escaping his parted lips. His ears are pinned to the sides of his head. Even his tail is pressed tight to his body. Every inch of him screams how much agony he's in. I wonder if I made the wrong choice to step in front of him. But I know I didn't. I would do it again if given the chance.

A shudder runs through me as he breaks himself from his stupor and lets out a roar. He whirls and charges to where Justin is crumpled on the grass.

I don't know how my ex is still alive. I shot him twice, and one of those times was in his stomach area. I think I read somewhere that someone can survive a bullet to the stomach for up to twenty-four hours. Anger pulses through my ghostly form. Never before this moment have I wished I'd taken a course on how to shoot a gun. Either way, I should've emptied the damn bullet chamber into the fucker to make sure he was dead.

Also, how am I conscious and thinking? It's almost like I'm moving on a different timeline than what I'm witnessing because all of that occurred to me in less than a second. I'm not watching everything in slow motion, but it does feel like my brain is firing far more effectively than it did when I was alive. How odd. I can process the scene playing out in front of me with perfect detail while also thinking about facts and figures.

Cambion is rushing toward Justin. I can make out every single detail of what's happening, including watching my Deer Boy grip Justin's head between his hands while his hoof presses down on the gunshot wound to Justin's stomach. I hear Justin's scream cut off as Cambion twists his head and rips it from his spine. He tosses it to the side and stands there, his hands covered in blood.

I have no idea how much time has passed. It's probably only a matter of seconds. I tear my ghostly gaze away from Justin's corpse and focus on my mate. He falls to his knees, whimpering sobs once again erupting from his chest as he crawls to my body and cradles it against him. Tears continue to stream down his face as he rocks my body back and forth.

But something odd is happening.

The bullet wound in my chest is...glowing. I don't think Cambion notices, so lost in his grief as he is. But there's a warmth blooming from my chest, spreading all the way to my fingers and toes. That's when I realize I can feel it. I'm not just watching anymore. The fiery heat continues to flow through my body. I feel myself changing, almost as though I'm being reshaped. It's pain, but not. It's both exultant and frightening.

Cambion lifts his head as the glow brightens, his eyes wide. He keeps hold of me as my body lights up like hot iron in a fire. I feel a strange sucking sensation, and then I can no longer see. I also don't have the sensation of floating any longer. I feel solid. Whole. Complete.

I blink open my eyes to Cambion's tear-stained, disbelieving gaze. His lips are parted in shock. His ears are still pinned back in a universal sign of distress. But his eyes...

"Mate?" The hope in his voice cracks my heart in two.

A smile stretches my lips. "Hi." A yelp escapes me as he crushes me to him, pulling me up into a partial sitting position. My face is pressed to the crook of his neck as he trembles against me. I wind my arms around him, squeezing him to me. "I don't know how, but I'm not dead," I mutter against his skin.

A laughing sob escapes him.

"Hey, hey. It's okay."

His voice is a low rumble against me. "I have mixed feelings on the matter."

I chuckle and cling to him tighter. "I don't understand what happened."

He pulls away then, his gaze stern. "You made me break my promise to keep you safe, Christine."

I'm once again stunned by what I see as I hold his gaze, his words not registering in my mind. "Cambion?"

He blinks at me before his gaze goes to my body. No, not my body. He's looking at his hands. He removes one from around me and stares at it, flexing his fingers over and over – fingers no longer tipped in claws. "It's broken."

"What is?"

"My curse."

I give him a soft, teary smile. "Is that why your eyes are green now?"

He gapes at me. "They're green?"

I cup his face and tilt my head. "Hmm."

Despite everything, a small smirk lifts the corner of his lips. "What?"

"You still have your shark teeth though."

He laughs as he presses his forehead to mine. "My mate, don't you ever fucking scare me like that again?"

I chuckle and kiss his cheek. "Seriously though." I pull away. "How am I alive? And how did we break your curse?"

A regal female voice flows from behind us. "Do you really want the answer to that question?"

CHAPTER TWENTY-SIX

CAMBION

I blink as the Faerie Queen steps out of a portal, her snow-white gown a stark contrast to the green and brown forest that surrounds us.

Christine huffs a surprised breath. "What the fuck?"

Queen Aine's lips tighten in disapproval. "Is that any way to address the Queen of Faerie?"

I snarl as I tighten my hold on Christine. "The last time I saw you, you felt it was necessary to curse my brethren and I."

"It was necessary."

By the powers, I *hate* the condescension that's always in her tone.

Christine shifts away from me and starts to stand. I want to hold on to her and never let her go again, but I know the Queen prefers deference when people speak to her. Which means both of us should be standing in a respectful manner despite the blood that covers us and the corpse lying on the ground behind us. I help my mate to her feet, keeping one arm around her waist. I also try to keep the sneering to a minimum as I speak. "Hundreds of years of punishment was enough to satisfy you, your Majesty?"

Either she doesn't understand the heavy sarcasm in my voice, or she's ignoring it. Either way, she inclines her head toward my mate, though her gaze stays focused on me. "You, of all the Forest Lords, needed to understand love and empathy. Without the curse, you would've met your anam cara and missed out on the opportunity to fulfill your deepest desire and longing."

I can't help the resentment that builds in my chest. "So you did this to help me?" She opens her mouth, but I cut her off. "Because I find it hard to believe that the Queen of Faerie did this out of the goodness of her heart and not because of some ulterior motive. The fae don't do anything for the sake of being nice or compassionate."

Queen Aine's lips lift in a silent snarl, her elongated canines gleaming in the shadows. Her arched ear flicks as swirls of green light dance along her fingertips. "Tread carefully, Forest Lord. You're still at my mercy despite the destruction of your curse."

Christine pinches my buttock, startling me. My disbelieving gaze goes to her, but her focus is on the Faerie Queen. "Please forgive my mate. He's a little cranky because he didn't get a nap today." She caresses my tail, sending shivers down my spine, as she continues. "Would you please explain how the curse was broken, and how this affects us now? Your Majesty?"

The Queen's gaze softens a bit as she eyes my mate. "For your sake, I will. You have a kind heart, child. Which doesn't surprise me, considering the fact that you fell in love so quickly with the narcissistic Deer Lord."

Christine pinches my ass again when I open my mouth to loose a retort.

Aine keeps her focus on the goddess beside me. "Each Forest Lord received a curse for a specific reason. Of course, that means each one has his own story to tell, so I will only focus on Cambion's curse. You see, Cambion was once the proud Deer Lord of the forest. He could shift into the most magnificent of stags, or he could traipse in the demi-human form you're so used to seeing. However," she levels her piercing gaze on me, "he is arrogant and narcissistic, prideful beyond measure.

"The specificity of his curse was that he, himself, could not break his curse. Only a human with a connection to his heart, who was willing to spill blood on his behalf, would free him and allow him to return to his former state of glory."

Even as she speaks the words, I can feel the connection to my stag once again. For hundreds of years, he has been nothing but a monster crawling beneath my skin. I have missed the glorious buck that stands head and shoulders above all other deer.

Christine continues, pulling me from my wayward thoughts. "So he's no longer a demon?"

"Not in the sense you believe demons to be, no. He is once again the pure Deer Lord of the forest. And he is no longer bound to any single territory."

My heart lifts at the thought, but my mate seems melancholy in a way I cannot describe. Her posture slumps. It's a minute movement, but I feel it as I hold her against me. I lean my forehead against her temple, careful of my antlers. "What is it, my heart? Why do you seem sad?"

I ignore the smug look on Aine's face. Why she felt the need to teach me empathy and emotion, I'll perhaps never know. But it brought me to mo anam cara. I'm not grateful to the Faerie Queen, exactly, but I do understand the process behind her thinking.

Christine sucks in a deep breath as she looks up at me. "You're immortal, right? At least, that's what all the romantasy books make it seem like. The demons and fae and elves and whatever else are immortal, and the poor human either has to become one of them or remain human and live a shortened life."

I can't help the chuckle that escapes my lips, even before she finishes her diatribe.

"What is so funny?"

I kiss her temple then, amused at her irritation. "Queen Aine failed to mention that part of the lifting of my curse includes granting you immortality."

My mate's shoulders stiffen. "Come again?"

Queen Aine smiles. A genuine smile, which unnerves me. "He doesn't lie, child. It would've been cruel for me to curse him until he found his soulmate only to leave her a mortal who would die one day."

I raise a brow. "The curse was cruel, Aine." She scowls at my casual use of her name. "You cannot deny that."

She waves me off. "My reasons are my own, Cambion. One day, you will understand, perhaps. But not this day."

Christine looks between us. "So I'm never going to die?"

I shake my head. "Not of old age." I frown as I look to the Queen. "I could have explained this to her. Why are you really here?"

"To give you a nudge." Aine holds out both arms in a placating gesture. "As well as ask for a boon."

"A boon." I hope she can hear the distaste in my tone. As though I owe here *anything*.

Aine tilts her head, her eyes predatory. "The Fox Demon is making choices that will endanger him and others." She raises her brows at me. "He needs guidance to help him break his own curse."

I sigh, rubbing my forehead. The novelty of having bare-tipped fingers hasn't worn off, and it almost distracts me from my answer. "I will look into it."

"Good." She smiles warmly at my mate. "Keep him in check, child. I'm certain that despite the breaking of his curse, he'll still be the arrogant creature he's always been." Before I can retort, Aine opens a portal and vanishes through it within the span of a heartbeat.

Christine sags against me in that moment. I catch her and pull her to me, turning her away from the corpse that lies only a few feet from us. I'll need to take care of that. I no longer have a desire to eat human flesh, so I will dispose of it in a different way. Along with the weapon.

I press another kiss to her temple. "What is it, my heart? Are you well?"

She blinks up at me. "I'm immortal."

I smile. "Yes. Forever stuck to my side, I'm afraid. Can you handle it, little human?"

She grins at me, trailing a finger down my chest. "I think the question is, can you handle having me glued to your side for all eternity?" I'm very distracted by her finger as it travels lower, cupping my sheath.

I growl as I pull her to me and cover her lips with mine, sliding my tongue inside the warm hollow of her mouth and lavishing her with a deep kiss of longing.

She moans as she winds her arms around me, her tongue dancing with mine. My cock starts to extrude against her, and I make no attempt to stop what's happening between us. I slide my hands into her hair, none of the strands snagging on my fingers since my claws are gone. I pull away just long enough to say three words. "Your house. Now."

CHAPTER TWENTY-SEVEN

CHRISTINE

I don't protest when Cambion picks me up. I wrap my legs around his waist and let him carry me to my back door, rubbing my hips against the bulge of his extruded dick. I try not to think about the blood that's currently congealing in my room. I'll think of it later. I don't focus on the fact that my ex is lying dead outside. I remind myself that he attacked us. We acted in self-defense.

I lose all train of thought the moment Cambion sets me on the couch and drops to his knees, his hooves clacking together behind him. "I'm going to feast on your pretty little cunt now, human."

Holy. Shit. "Okay."

He unbuttons my jeans at an excruciating pace. I lift my hips so he can slide them, along with my panties, to my ankles.

Somehow, he manages to remove my shoes and pants all at the same time. My focus doesn't linger on that though, not as his hands spread my legs and his tongue goes to my sex, licking me from base to clit. "Mmm," he growls against me. "So wet for me."

And I swear it's like he's never gone down on me before. His tongue twirls around my clit as a finger slides deep inside my pussy. I arch, gripping the couch cushions behind my head as he finger fucks me.

"I've wanted to do this since the first time I tasted you, my goddess." He slides a second finger inside me.

My breath comes out in gasping pants as he works me into a frenzy. I think I cry out his name, or some garbled version of it, as I come hard enough that I can't breathe. All I feel is the sensation of his clawless fingers still pumping into me, his tongue lapping up my juices. He draws out my orgasm for what feels like five minutes before I'm yanked off the couch by my hips.

I lie on my back, looking up at my mate. His gorgeous, emerald eyes hold mine. Eyes that convey so much affection, yearning, love. We pause, though my lungs still heave. I take the moment to trace the contours of his beautifully masculine face with my fingertips, gliding up to his soft deer ears. He closes his eyes then as I trace the furry outline of those sensitive ears before moving to his antlers. I grip them and pull his head down toward me.

I expect him to crush my mouth beneath his, but the kiss he lavishes on me is the most tender kiss we've ever shared. Sweet enough to make my eyes prick with emotion.

"Never leave me again," he whispers against my mouth. "I won't survive losing my heart." He trails his lips to my neck. "I would die a slow, soulless death without you."

One of my hands goes to the back of his head, the other clutches his shoulders. "I love you too."

My words must unleash something in him because before I can grasp what he's doing, he uses his sharp teeth to rip down the center of my shirt. I gasp as his hands cup my breasts, his thumbs kneading my nipples. He draws one into his mouth, suckling and teasing. I grip his antlers even as I moan. "Doing things...a little backwards, are...we?"

He growls, moving his mouth to my other nipple before he kisses his way back up to my mouth. I only have time to spread my thighs before the ridged head of his cock is teasing my entrance. "No," he answers me. His elbows rest on either side of me as he cups my face in his hands. "I'm just reminding myself that you're here." He inches into my pussy a little more. "That you're mine."

I whimper as he presses into the hilt. Being filled by him makes me feel alive. Like I'm home. "And you're mine."

His eyes soften as he kisses me, pulling out and thrusting back in with exquisite slowness. My hands slide down the skin of his back to the fur over his ass. I hold him there as we move together. The intensity builds and builds until neither of us can stand it any longer and he's pounding into me, grunting with each thrust. I think I leave nail marks down his back as I come around him with a scream. It doesn't take him long to follow, my name on his lips.

He collapses on top of me, his breathing labored, though he still holds most of his weight on his elbows. His deer tail flicks against my hand as he presses his face into the crook of my neck, once again shrinking his antlers into those cute little fawn nubs. I hold him against me, so sated I don't feel like I can move. His cock pulses deep inside me as he lifts his head just enough to rest it against my forehead.

"You are my heart." His throat is thick. "Forever."

I brush my lips against his. "Forever."

EPILOGUE

CAMBION

I graze in the front yard of Christine's house as her best friend's car pulls into the driveway. I lift my head as any deer would, keeping my ears trained in her direction as she gets out of the car. She admires me for a moment, probably assuming she's seeing a normal stag. I swish my tail and back up a step or two, feigning fear. Since she is a soft-hearted human, she holds up her hands and tiptoes to the front door, using the spare key Christine gave her. With a last glance of me, she goes inside, calling for my mate.

If I were in my half-human form, I'd snort my amusement. As it is, I make my way to the open window of the kitchen, where I know the two women will sit and enjoy some hot tea and freshly baked cupcakes while they chat. Of course I'll be eavesdropping. Why wouldn't I? I make sure to keep my head bent as though I'm grazing, just in case of a passing car.

Kathleen's voice drifts toward me from the kitchen table. "That deer has been outside your house a few times now."

Christine's golden laughter ripples over my fur. "Yeah. I've been putting out corn, and he kind of sticks around."

I snort, satisfied when I hear her choke on her tea.

Over the last week, we've gone round and round the discussion of whether or not to tell Kathleen of my existence. For now, my insistence wins out. I will be kept a secret.

My mate is quiet for a moment before she asks the question that I know is burning a hole in her mind. "So what did the police ask you when they came by?"

I lift my head so I can peer in the window. Kathleen is facing away from me, though I see my mate's eyes sparkle in my direction for a moment. I grin at her, giving her a wink. Her eyes widen. She's never seen me give human expressions in this form. It's quite amusing, and I think I'll do that more often.

Kathleen sips on her tea, shrugging. "They asked if I knew why he was in town since phone records showed I was the last person he called. I told them the truth. That he called asking about you, but I hadn't seen him at all." I wish I could see her facial expression. "I would like to know why his car is in town, but he's nowhere to be found. Even his belongings are still at the hotel he was staying at twenty miles from here."

Christine's eyes harden. "I can't believe he came all the way out here to stalk me." I notice she's careful not to say anything further. She told me she didn't want to lie to her best friend, and would need to tread carefully over any conversation they had.

Of course, the insufferable, useless male left his car parked in front of a business before he walked to Christine's house. The owner called the police to report the car since it'd been parked in the same spot for several days. The police conducted an investigation that yielded no results. He had no current lover, and as far as my mate knows, he didn't keep in touch with his family. We'd disposed of the rug he'd bled all over, and cleaned up the house, by the time Christine was questioned by police a couple days after I ripped his head from his shoulders.

The day it happened, Christine was shaken up in so many ways, her anxiety in full force. Even after making love to her on her living room floor, she didn't have a good day. I spent the rest of the day comforting her however she needed until she eventually fell asleep around sunset. She'd fallen asleep in my arms, and though I was reluctant to let her go at all, I knew I needed to take care of the asshole's body.

I carried his body, along with his severed head, deeper into the woods, outside of my territory boundary. And, as Queen

Aine requested, I found the Fox Demon Lord to have a little chat with him. Could I help it if we happened to be close enough to Justin's body that the Fox Demon lost control and his brain turned to goo? At least no one will ever find the fucker. It's more than he deserves. He should've been left to rot until his bones turned to dust.

☐Christine has been sick over his death despite the fact that she only acted in self-defense. I wish I could take that burden from her. She doesn't need to hold onto it. He attacked her. And I'm the one that killed him. If anyone should feel guilty, it should be me. Will I ever feel guilty? Absolutely not.

☐I tune back in to the conversation in the kitchen.

☐Kathleen shudders a bit. "Speaking of stalkers, there's something I haven't told you." She pauses, and Christine's blue eyes widen a bit. "I'm being watched. I think."

☐Christine frowns. "What do you mean?"

☐There's another pause. My ears flick with impatience. "I feel like something...not-human is following me around."

☐My mate eyes me as Kathleen studies the cupcake in her hand. "What do you mean?"

☐"I knew you'd think I was crazy."

☐Christine reaches out to touch Kathleen's hand. "I didn't say that. I asked what you meant."

☐Kathleen licks at the frosting on her cupcake, her gaze still avoidant of my mate.

Christine takes the moment to lick the frosting on her own cupcake, her eyes never leaving mine. Then a devious little grin crosses her face. My wicked goddess knows exactly what she's doing as she proceeds to use her finger to scoop even more frosting off the cake and suck it off with great relish. Oh, she'll be punished for that later. She smirks as if she can read my thoughts.

Kathleen sighs, snagging my mate's attention again. "Look, I know it's crazy, but I swear to you, I saw some kind of fox dog thing following me the other night."

My stomach jolts. *He failed to mention* that *little tidbit when we had our chat.*

Christine's brows rise. "When?"

"When I was driving home. I looked in the rearview mirror and I saw this...creature standing on its hind legs. But it had a fox face with a human torso. The back legs were foxlike, I think. It was hard to tell in the dark. But I could see it had a tail. A tail, Chris!"

"You said it was dark out?" I hear the skepticism in her voice, though I know she believes Kathleen. How could she not since she knows we exist?

Kathleen nods. "Yes, but I know what I saw. I even slammed on the brakes, but when I looked back, it was gone."

Christine taps her chin for a moment. "Have you seen it since?"

"No. The only time was two days ago."

Hmm. Perhaps I need to go have another little chat with the Fox Demon. But later. I'd rather sit here and spy on my beautiful female through the window.

The women sit and talk for a little while longer, devouring cupcakes and laughing. When Kathleen finally stands and takes her mug to the sink, I know she's about to leave. I meander out of sight before she leaves the house. It wouldn't do for her to start guessing things that aren't her business. As soon as she's down the road, I shift to my half-human form and make my way in through the back door, careful to lock it. I will never leave the damn thing unlocked again.

Christine is already washing dishes in the sink. I come up behind her, though it's impossible to sneak up on her since my hooves sound like thunder on her wood floor. She leans back against me as I put my arms around her, resting my chin on top of her head. "Hello, Deer Boy."

"Hello, little human."

She squeals as I tickle her stomach and ribs, thrashing in my hold. She manages to wrench away from me and I let her go, giving her five seconds before I go after her. She tries to shut her bedroom door in my face. When that doesn't work, she rubs her dish-wet hands over my chest. I growl and tackle her to the ground, careful to cage her in so she doesn't hurt herself.

☐She breaks into breathless laughter at our antics. I kiss her nose. "You're so adorable."

☐"Shut up," she giggles. *Giggles.*

☐I nip her nose. "So apparently, I need to go have a chat with...what did you call him? Fox Boy?"

☐"Apparently. Do you think that's what Queen Aine meant? That he was stalking my best friend and we needed to intervene before he –"

☐"Maybe," I interrupt. "But right now?" I roll her so she's pinned beneath me. Her hips squirm against my sheath, but I don't budge. "You gave me a show with that damn cupcake, and I think it's time you make good on that promise."

☐She smirks at me, her beautiful blue eyes holding mine. "Do you want me to suck your dick, Deer Boy?"

☐My cock threatens to extrude at her filthy words. I lean down so my lips are at her ear and nip her earlobe, just hard enough to send shivers up and down her spine. "Only after I make you come so hard, you forget your own name," I growl.

☐I trail my lips to her mouth and kiss her, my tongue gliding along the seam of her lips so I can devour her sweet taste. She moans into my mouth, her tongue dancing and writhing against mine.

☐I pull away after a moment, pressing my forehead to hers, reveling in the fact that after centuries of loneliness and longing, I'm home. "My heart," I whisper.

□She cups my face in her hands, tracing my cheeks with her thumbs. "Forever."

AUTHOR'S NOTE

Thank you so much for reading my first monster romance! I adore Cambion's and Christine's story, and I hope that you do too. If this is your introduction to my books, welcome. I'm so happy to have you here!

I'd been thinking about writing a monster romance for quite awhile, and I actually *have* written an outline for a minotaur romance. But then I was introduced to Hazbin Hotel, and found I have a soft spot for several of the characters. I was also rereading *The Cruel Prince* by Holly Black at the same time. Cardan has long been one of my favorite broody book boyfriends, and my husband likes it when I read some of my favorite books to him. I started thinking, "What if I were to mix narcissistic Alastor with lonely Cardan?" And BAM! Cambion was created in my head.

If you liked this novella, pretty please leave a review on Amazon and/or Goodreads. It really does help me out! I sometimes sneak a peak, and it makes my little author heart happy when people leave reviews. I know I shouldn't, but my nosy ass can't help itself.

This novella has spawned an idea for six other books, one for each of the Demon Forest Lords. I have a vague story outlined for each one, including an MM story for one of them! They will take place in different forests throughout the United States, aside from Fox Boy of course. I will be writing these novellas sporadically in-between my other novels. As you can probably guess from the story, Fox Boy and Kathleen will star in the second *Demon Lords of the Forest* novella. I can't wait for you to get to know both of them better. I don't have a release date yet since I have other writing obligations to fulfill. I'm also hoping to get some art commissioned for my Demon Lords. Keep an eye out on my socials for that!

Next up, I will be releasing the fourth and final book in my *Assassins of Quadrania* series. It will come out in late August 2024. I will also be compiling all four of those books in one Omnibus edition that will include extra artwork throughout. I have some commissions for that series that I've been keeping a secret.

After that, I will be writing the third book in my *Immar and Stauros* high fantasy trilogy, which is long overdue. The first two books in that trilogy, *Dueling Fates* and *Divided Fates*, are getting new covers courtesy of my publishing company, Between the Lines Publishing.

Thanks again for reading this little novella. I had so much fun writing it! Until the next release, best to you, my monster fudgers!

SOCIAL MEDIA INFO:

Instagram: @thestephmarieallen

Threads: @thestephmarieallen

TikTok: AuthorStephanieMAllen

ALSO BY STEPHANIE M. ALLEN

<u>Assassins of Quadrania Saga</u>: mature (18+) new adult fantasy romance series

Heiress of Sun and Blood

King of Ice and Misery

Master of Intent and Illusion

Dynasty of Beasts and Darkness (Releasing August 2024)

Assassins of Quadrania Special Omnibus Edition (Releasing December 2024)

<u>Demon Lords of the Forest:</u> mature (18+) monster romance novella series

Taming the Deer Demon

Training the Fox Demon <u>(Releasing late 2024 or early 2025)</u>

Future Book – Cougar Demon

Future Book – Wolf Demon

Future Book – Bat Demon

Future Book – Bear Demon

Future Book – Bison Demon

※※※※ ※※※※

<u>The Harmony Saga:</u> young adult portal fantasy series

Harmony

Sealed Shadows

Clashing Fury

Prevailing Light

Harmony Saga Omnibus Edition (Releasing Summer 2024)

※※※※ ※※※※

<u>Immar and Stauros Trilogy:</u> high fantasy trilogy

Dueling Fates (Re-releasing 2024)

Divided Fates (Re-releasing 2024)

Destructive Fates (Releasing 2025)

Made in the USA
Columbia, SC
11 July 2024

38236265R00119